One Silent Night

Janice Chaffee

HARVEST
HOUSE
PUBLISHERS

EUGENE, OREGON 97402

CCM
BOOKS

NASHVILLE, TENNESSEE 37205

ONE SILENT NIGHT
Copyright © 2000 by Janice Chaffee
Published by Harvest House Publishers
Eugene, Oregon 97402 and
CCM Books, a division of CCM Communications
Nashville, TN 37205

Library of Congress Cataloging-in-Publication Data

Chaffee, Janice.
    One silent night / Janice Chaffee.
      p. cm.
    ISBN 0-7369-0496-4
    1. Christmas stories. I. Title.

PN6071.C6 C42 2000
242'.335—dc21   00-033484

To Barbara Roberts Pine

editor of my words
mentor of my life
example of my soul

Acknowledgments

I am grateful to Terry Glaspey and Carolyn McCready at Harvest House Publishers and Roberta Croteau at CCM Books for their willingness to take on this project—even with such a short deadline!

Dawn Gates, Rachel Murphy, and Kelley Tucker typed out precise and thorough *(cough, giggle, sigh)* transcriptions. They literally rescued me from a sea of cassettes.

This book would not exist without the women who trusted me enough to tell their stories. It was my privilege to sit in their presence, to record their laughter and tears, and to print their private lives on paper. What an honor to be in the company of such honest and exemplary women.

My mother gave me life, a love for Christmas, and the best gifts a five-year-old could ever hope for.

Elliott and Taylor—I gave you life and you gave me stress, gray hair, and sleepless nights, as well as real laughter, pure love, and a pride that knows no limit.

Jim—the day I met you was a most Memorial Day.

Contents

So let the ages wonder
that the angel bore the seed
that the virgin received through her ear,
and, believing in her heart, bore fruit.

—Venatius Fortunatus, Latin poet

Our Link with the Eternal

Janice's Story

⚜

My flight departed Los Angeles on a sunny day in June and fourteen hours later landed in Aukland, New Zealand. My Kiwi family greeted me warmly in a cold, howling wind and slushy downpour of rain. I knew before I left, of course, that I was flying out of one season and into another. Still, stepping off the plane, I was surprised by the sensational blast of January-like cold. A great gust of reality blew away all my expectations.

My intention to visit in New Zealand for just a few weeks stretched into a year and a half. The longer my stay, the more aware I became of my fallacious correlation between seasons and holidays. The seasons progressed in a sequential order, but in all the wrong months! A chilly July fourth passed without stars and stripes and fireworks, August lengthened into warmer days, and September blossomed into spring. October's roads weren't littered with bronze and burgundy leaves and November brought no pilgrims or thankful harvest feasts. But—December did bring Christmas.

It didn't *seem* like Christmas to me, wearing a T-shirt, shorts, and sandals while arranging a nativity set and decorating a tree. It didn't seem like December either, sweltering in hazy heat measured by Celsius rather than Fahrenheit. On Christmas Day, instead of opening cold-weather gifts of sweaters, coats, and flannel pajamas, my Kiwi presents included a neon pink beach towel (from friends who knew I hate pink), ornate teaspoons (for the ever-present cup of hot tea), and a pile of books to read at the beach during summer vacation. That's when I realized that so much of what I considered essentially Christmas was, in fact, seasonal and cultural.

In New Zealand, I lived in a different climate, with a different family that celebrated different traditions. Was Christmas Day any less meaningful or significant to me? No. Just different. Red and green poinsettias were conspicuously absent, and instead of my favorite pecan pie for dessert, everyone clamored for a piece of the beautiful white pavlova garnished with amber passion fruit. However, one thing remained the same: the story. God gave the gift of a Savior, delivered of Mary and laid in a manger. The shepherds, the star, the angels, the wise men—the story didn't change.

Like my American and New Zealand families, many people around the world celebrate Christmas with relatives and friends crowded around tables loaded with platters of food, generations jammed elbow to elbow on extra chairs brought in from the kitchen. Beautifully wrapped presents are piled under festive trees, and the scent of fresh pine floats through the house. Bursts of children's laughter and a constant stream of adult chatter are underscored by the familiar crooning of "I'm Dreaming of a White Christmas" and classic holiday carols. Christmas is the occasion of loving reunions and repeated traditions, captured in expanding family photo albums. For some. But not for all.

The majority of the world's people who celebrate Christmas experience something less than Rockwellian happiness and togetherness. For some, Christmas is just another lonely day, like the day before and the one to follow. For others, the season of good cheer delivers painful memories of uninvited loss and change. To many, it's a reminder that life did not turn out quite as expected. In many homes, the only illumination of Christmas comes from twinkle lights, often shadowed by depression. From sand castles to snow angels, there are as many experiences of Christmas as there are people who observe it. But before I lived in New Zealand, I hadn't seen the celebration of Christ's birth from any perspective but my own.

Collecting women's stories for this book made me realize again the value of differing viewpoints. The women's ages range from 20 to 96, and their experiences took place in settings as varied as a Navajo reservation, the Far East, a parsonage, a prison, a homeless mission, and the stage of the Grammy Awards. I was struck by the similar core of each story: Despite obvious differences among them, each woman told of the significant influence of Christ's birth one silent night.

My impression of the very first Christmas has been shaped by the beloved carol, "Silent Night," which paints the first noel as quiet and calm, a holy family serenely gathered under a brilliant star, serenaded by a heavenly choir singing "Alleluia." Joseph Mohr wrote the lyric in 1816 and for nearly two hundred years his musical portrait of Christ's birth has colored our collective Christmas imagery. But I'm convinced that "cacophony" better describes the reality of that holy night.

In my imagination, I see hundreds, perhaps thousands, of travelers jostling against one another in the narrow, crowded streets of Bethlehem, elbowing their way to ancestral homes and to anxious relatives. Competing vendors shout the value of their wares in dissonance with street musicians who play in hope for a few tossed coins. Tired animals bray for relief from their shifting burdens. Odors of dung and sweat, of baking bread and roasting lamb waft through dusty air. Mothers and fathers clutch hungry, crying children and whisper the promise to soon be there. Shouts of greeting, murmurs of political resistance, the metallic clang of Roman weapons, brawling and revelry bounce across rutted streets and against earthen city walls. The night of Christ's birth was anything but silent.

Imagine the frustration Joseph and Mary must have felt, pushing through the throbbing crowd, anxious to finish their

90-mile walk from Nazareth and eager to find a place to stay. Imagine the rush of silence as they stepped into the temporary shelter of the barn shared with common creatures. They inhaled the fragrant hay dust and the pungent musk of wool and feathers, then wearily collapsed onto mounded pillows of straw. Weak with exhaustion, eyes closed in relief, their ears tuned to the quiet rhythm of a cow chewing her cud, the rustle of roosting chickens, the slurping of a nursing lamb.

Inside this coarse sanctuary, Mary's brief rest was broken by pain rippling through her body. Her moaning was the only sound attending the difficult task of birth. Then, in a sliver of silence, she heard the scratchy, infant cry of God. Mary cradled her perfect son to her breast, and in that moment of fulfilled promise, attempted to reconcile the reality of her stark surroundings to the expectation she held in her heart.

Blessed among women? Was this what God intended? A Savior in a stable? Her expectation of this night must have been terribly confused by the reality. But Mary's story confirms that Christmas is exactly what it claims and seldom what we expect. Christmas *is* the celebration of the incarnation of God. But who expected his arrival in a barn, a feed trough for his crib? Mary thought she knew *what* was going to happen, only she had no idea *how* God would bring it to pass. And generations of women later, our thoughts mirror hers. God's promises to us are kept, but not always as we expect. God is with us—Emmanuel—through life's inextricable weaving of joy with sorrow, belief with doubt, peace with fear, expectation with reality.

When I flew to New Zealand, I knew I was headed for winter, enough to pack sweaters and gloves. Still, when I arrived, I was stunned by the sting of icy air that met me. In my mind, I expected a change of seasons, but I wasn't ready for the physical sensation of numbing wind and freezing rain. Mary knew she was going to have a child, even that she would name him Jesus, but I doubt she was expecting the cold barbs of criticism or the blasts of confusion.

The whole of Christ's story, the crucifixion and the resurrection, began with the power of the incarnation. How does his miraculous entry into humanity affect the story of our lives—our past, our present, and our future? My pastor, Dr. Tom Walker, once said, "The past informs our present and prepares us for the future." The Christmas story, the greatest story of all time, is humankind's link to the eternal God. The Christ Child in the setting of the nativity embodied a prophecy fulfilled, a present hope, and a promise for the future.

This book is a collection of true stories of Christmas. It is not about avoiding stress in December's frenetic schedule or sharing helpful decorating tips; it is not about planning menus, wrapping gifts, or sending cards. It records the voices of women who, in various stages of life, grasped the eternal, knelt in adoration, and experienced the meaning of the incarnation. These women began their spiritual journeys to the resurrected Christ with a step toward the infant in the manger. They found hope in the pain of despair, happiness in a cacophonous season of commerce, and contentment in the realities of life. They found constancy in the unexpected because of their faith in a baby in a manger. Like Mary, they heard the voice of God one silent night.

one

Tamales and Traditions
Around a Tree

Jaci Velasquez is part all-American girl, part pop-star, and seemingly unaware of the power of her trademark waist-length dark hair, almond-shaped eyes, and natural beauty. Her youthful energy and free-spirited nature disarm and charm everyone in her presence.

Signed to a recording contract at age 15, Jaci is Christian music's top-selling debut artist of all time. Now at age 20, she's sold millions of albums, won several Dove awards, and written her first book, *Heavenly Place*. Her very first Spanish album was nominated for the Best Latin Pop Performance Grammy Award.

No matter where she is, Jaci never meets a stranger, just a new friend. She moves with ease between secular and sacred, contemporary and traditional, Anglo and Spanish worlds without losing sight of what's important to her— family. She feels at home wherever she finds herself, but never more so than with family in New Mexico. During the interview for this story about Christmas, Jaci and her mother, Diana, laughed and filled in each other's sentences that began, "Remember the time when... "

JACI'S STORY

*W*hen I hear people say, "You can choose your friends, but you can't choose your relatives," it makes me sad. I'm only twenty years old and haven't been through a lot in life yet, but I'm old enough to understand the value of my family. Besides life, and the life through Jesus Christ, the best gift in the world is family.

Most of my friends describe their families as their mom, dad, brothers, sisters, and sometimes grandparents. When we say family, we mean *everybody*! Our mom, dad, all *their* brothers and sisters, all our grandparents and great-grandparents, and our brothers and sisters. Plus our cousins—first, second, and third— are just like brothers and sisters. And when anyone gets married, their husband or wife becomes family too. It's cool to have so many people in life to depend on, who look just like you, who can look at each other and say, "We definitely get this nose from our Grandma." That's what I call family!

We go to New Mexico every year for Christmas and my relatives just see me as Jaci, the cousin. I love it. Sometimes an aunt or uncle or another cousin will say they're proud of me, but they don't go on and on. I don't have to talk about music stuff or my professional life. I do dishes and clean up like everybody else. I'm just one of the girls. That's probably one of the most special things about going home. I can just be Jaci.

Being in a large family adds so much to life, so much happiness, a sense of belonging. It makes hard things bearable to know you have so many shoulders to lean on and so many shoulders to cry on. Shoulders of different ages and shapes. When we may not have very many friends, we know we have family.

I guess because there are so many of us and we're all so close, I forget that out in the bigger world I'm considered "different" than the average American person. In reality, there is no average American person and I'm surprised when others react to me because of the way I look or because of my last name. Many people seem quick to judge others by appearance, by race, by style, by accent. I wish that weren't true, but it is.

I don't see myself as being different—maybe because I have an entire family just like me! But other people see the way we do things as different or even strange. Especially when I talk about how we celebrate Christmas. We serve some traditional foods, like ham, mashed potatoes and gravy, corn, and salad, but we also feast on tamales, posole, red and green chili, tortillas, and sopapillas. Our non-traditional meal scares some of my friends: "What is *that*? What kind of food are we eating?" I laugh and tell them those are *our* traditional Christmas dishes—the tamales and the chili that burns your mouth if you eat it the wrong way. Even our desserts, such as biscochito—shortbread-type cookies with anise seeds—reflect our heritage, though my mom also bakes the best apple and pumpkin pies. My mother is a great cook and she always makes this really hot red chili with pork and corn, thick like stew, and we pour it over mashed potatoes instead of gravy. It's weird, but it's a family thing. And I love it.

Every Christmas, my family (*all* of us!) gathers in New Mexico at Nana Kate's, my grandmother's house. That's been our tradition forever. Mom is one of seven children, and they all show up with their spouses and children and grandchildren. It makes for a very interesting, loud, and crowded day! A few years ago, everyone brought all their own family's gifts, but the packages took up so much space that there was absolutely no room for people! Because it was so overwhelming, we decided not to do that anymore.

We tried exchanging names one year and that didn't work either. We all want to give everybody something, even if it's just a coloring book and crayons for the littlest kids. We don't give expensive gifts, just simple ones. For us, the biggest and best gift of all is being together at Nana Kate's.

She is so amazing and so much fun we sometimes call her "Super Granny." We all love her. She plays with us and lets us get mad when she beats us at board games. She wrestles on the floor with the little kids and gets fierce in snowball fights. If someone is coming or going, they can count on getting smacked with a snowball. Then it escalates until all the adults and all the kids are in the front yard, including Nana, yelling, ducking, throwing snow, and laughing until we can't breathe.

My immediate family is usually the first to arrive in New Mexico. While we're waiting for everyone else to get there, we make luminarias, those paper bags filled with sand and a small candle. Aunts and uncles and kids make them together, four generations preparing light for Christmas. We set them around the driveway and make a design in the yard. Then after dark, we light the candles and admire our handiwork.

Another of our traditions is that we all pile into a couple of cars and drive around town to see the Christmas lights. We save one big house on the edge of town for last. The owners decorate their entire hill and you can see it from miles away. Every year they add something to the incredible scene, and it's always so much fun to discover the new part and see the stuff they've had for years. I have to admit, though, that there is nothing like the luminarias—the yellowy candlelight glowing through dozens of paper bags in the darkness. I love coming home to see them, year after year.

By Christmas Eve the entire family is together. Some of them attend Mass or a program at a local church, or we all go together to a midnight service. I always love the sight of Mary riding in on a donkey and am moved at the beauty of a live baby in the manger. Sometimes, we decide to stay at home and watch a Christmas special on television, just waiting for everyone to come in so we can open presents.

Everyone's very first gift is from my grandmother—a little brown paper bag filled with an apple and an orange, nuts, and Christmas candy. There are so many bags lined up under the tree! I love those bags. They're tradition. My mom used to get one from her grandmother and now I get one from mine. I can't wait until I have children and they get one from my mom. It's a simple gift, but it represents such love.

Then mad chaos begins when we open all the rest of the gifts—oh, my gosh! The noise in the house is amazing—little kids shouting and running and people talking non-stop in Spanish and English. Of course, everyone is eating all the time and drinking eggnog topped with whipped cream and nutmeg. I don't know if that tradition is Spanish or English or German or what, but we love it! We hang out, talk, and laugh, play music and games, and eat all night long. Together—as a family.

Of course, it's inevitable that the family stories get told and re-told year after year. Even though I used to get embarrassed, I couldn't wait until someone told one of "my" stories. I was about two or three when I got my first doll. It was one of those big ones, almost as big as me. I ripped open the box, but couldn't get the doll out since it was fastened down with wire. I was so happy and in such a hurry to love her, I just climbed in the box and laid down. I don't remember doing that at all, but it seems as though I do because I've heard the story so many times.

Even though I've heard the original Christmas story so many times, it's still wonderful to hear it again—the angels, the shepherds, the wise men bringing gifts to the baby in the manger. There's such comfort in knowing the story will be told again and again and that it will never change.

God promised to be faithful to all generations and He is. It's up to us to pass on the story of Christmas, just the way my family passes on the tradition of red chili on mashed potatoes. It's one thing to pass on traditions of food, but it's more important to pass on a tradition of truth that affects eternity. The younger adults and the children see the example of faith in the older generation, in mothers and fathers and aunts and uncles and brothers and sisters and cousins—first, second, or third—and take it as their own. Our tradition of lighting luminarias reminds us that Jesus came as the Light of the world. Passing out brown bags filled with fruit and candy reminds us that every gift comes from the Father of lights. When we are together, laughing and teasing and playing in the snow, we are reminded that the people of God are called a family.

It all started with the birth of a boy in a town filled with traditions. His family was small and probably quiet the night of his birth. My family is large and we're never very quiet. Our families may be different, but we both received the same thing: a baby in a manger, the perfect gift from God.

two

A Fragrant Segment of Love

Nicole C. Mullen is a shining light, both on and off the platform. Vivacious and relentlessly enthusiastic, she radiates happiness through her gorgeous smile and sparkling eyes. A thick mane of hundreds of braids hang nearly to her waist and gently sway to the rhythm of her music. She is a striking presence.

Now a solo recording artist, Nicole polished her talents as a background vocalist, songwriter, dancer, and choreographer, frequently touring with Amy Grant and Michael W. Smith. Nicole wrote "On My Knees," recorded by Jaci Velasquez, and was the first African-American to win a Dove award for Song of the Year. Very young fans recognize her voice as the featured artist on the "Larry Boy Theme Song" from *VeggieTales* and as "Serena the Cat" on the YO! Kids video series.

Nicole sees her career as a musical way to tell the world, "I want you to know the Christ I know." Off the platform, she pursues that mission. She and her husband, David, are youth leaders in their church, and every week she can be found tutoring inner-city kids. Her own two children occupy center stage at home, but Christ occupies the center of Nicole's life.

Nicole's Story

Every year, my husband and I alternate our Christmas celebration between our families, the Mullens and the Colemans. One recent Coleman year, I was more than ready to spend time laughing with my sisters, to relax in the familiarity of my childhood home, and to hang out with my mom and dad. I smiled in anticipation all the way to Cincinnati.

I was not disappointed. As usual, Christmas with my family started on Christmas Eve. After dinner, my mom and dad, my brother, my sisters and their husbands, and all the grandchildren settled in the living room to listen to Dad read the Christmas story from the book of Luke. We sang songs, exchanged gifts, ate more food than anyone should, and laughed and talked until there was nothing left but sleep. On Christmas Day, keeping to tradition, we visited aunts, uncles, cousins, old friends, and grandparents. This year, like all the ones before, I especially wanted to see Papa. Only I knew this visit would be different.

Napolean Coleman, Sr. was a fun grandpa. Round and jolly, his chocolate brown-eyes twinkled with good humor, his smooth skin glowed like cocoa butter, and his thick hair was more and more salt than pepper. He loved taking pictures, and he loved being with the family he captured on film. I remember him jogging beside me as I learned to ride my first two-wheeler. Every time I ran toward him, his wide, toothy smile lit up his face and my life. As a little girl, I waited to hear my favorite words: "Ah, here comes Bubbles."

Papa had no more than a sixth-grade education, but he was a dynamic self-taught educator and energetic pastor. A Pentecostal preacher, he shouted and danced and waved his handkerchief to make the stories of Scripture come alive. The Bible was his favorite book and his favorite saying was, "If you ain't got no joy, you ain't got no strength; and if you ain't got no strength, you ain't got no joy."

When I was just two years old, Papa took my two sisters and me up to the platform at the front of his church and told us to sing. Although I was a little shy, I obeyed my Papa. We sang:

> *Everywhere, take this message everywhere*
> *Tell 'em that Jesus loves and he cares*
> *and all of your burdens he's willing to share*
> *Take it everywhere, take this message everywhere.*

In between each line, Papa cheered us on. "Sing, children!" "That's right, baby!" From the time I was a toddler, Papa has told me, "Bubbles, keep singing for Jesus." And not only me. Papa was just as encouraging to my sisters and all my cousins. It never failed. If we were in his church, we were on his platform singing or playing hymns of our faith. We were anxious to please him, but we were also thrilled to receive a silver dollar at the end of the service! We didn't consider these coins as payment for sitting through his sermons, but as tokens of his love for us.

Papa always seemed the same, wearing a white shirt, suspenders, gray pants, and a big smile. When I first moved to Nashville and plunged into the work of my adult life, I got the news that Papa was admitted to a nursing home. I was stunned.

My Papa in a nursing home? It seemed impossible that a man of his vitality could ever need such a thing.

I thought of Papa often and was eager to see him when David and I returned to Ohio that Christmas. I knew it would be weird to visit him in a new setting, in unfamiliar surroundings. I wasn't sure what to expect on Christmas Day when most of our family piled into the car for the short drive to Papa's new home. But I did expect to hear, "Ah, here comes Bubbles."

The first part of our journey took us over the same roads my sisters and I took to school on the city bus when we were little girls. I remembered back to a particularly hard year when every morning, as soon as we got on, some older girls on the back of the bus would yell out, "Here comes 'Homemade.' " We were not the cutest, nor the most fashionable of kids. The girls would continue to mock us. They railed on our hair, our clothes, or whatever else they could think of to embarrass us. I hated what they were doing but knew I couldn't control the situation or make them stop.

At those awful moments, I had the power of choice. I could become bitter or better from anything in life, even their taunts. Because of the example of people like my grandfather, I chose the latter. Papa lived the truth that it's better to bless than to curse, it's better to give than it is to receive. Even back then, I knew that hate often "shows off," but following my Papa's lifestyle, I learned that it's amazing what love can do.

My eyes were misty as we pulled into the unfamiliar parking lot of Papa's residential home, a plain facility, sparsely decorated with outdoor holiday lights. I followed my parents through a maze of corridors and entered a sterile room. At first, I didn't recognize the frail man leaning against the metal frame of a wheelchair. His skin had paled to a lighter shade of cocoa. I had to adjust my memory of him to the reality before me. Strong arms that once held me now rested weakly in his lap. Not a flicker of recognition crossed his face, not a sound of welcome escaped his lips. My heart seized with shock and sadness. I despised what Alzheimer's had done to my Papa.

My dad, Papa's oldest son, called out, "Merry Christmas, Dad! We've brought you a present." He reached into a small gift bag. He did not pull out a shirt and tie; Papa had no place to wear such clothes. He did not pull out an electronic gadget or some new power tool; Papa had no need of such things. Dad pulled out tangerines, glossy and vibrant orange against the drab surroundings.

My first thought was, what an odd thing to give to Papa. Then I realized the gift was perfect. He loved tangerines. My dad knew that even in this season of life, tangerines would penetrate his mind as a nostalgic treat. But they were much more than that. They were a reminder to us that this failing man was still the patriarch we knew. He was still Napolean Coleman, Sr. He was still Papa who loved tangerines. With the grace and dignity of someone holding a bar of gold, my dad held a tangerine and carefully peeled the thin-skinned fruit. Its acidic fragrance filled the room like incense. Dad gently pulled the sections apart and presented a small piece to his father. With a smile and a nod, the transfer was complete.

Papa smelled a sliver of his past and his eyes brightened in remembrance. He accepted the gift from my dad's outstretched hand. For a moment, my Papa was back. Papa, the man who passed on a legacy of godliness to those he fathered, to those he adopted, to those he loved. Papa, who gave more than he received and considered himself blessed by the experience. Papa, who believed that life and love were the greatest gifts of all.

I stood there, a young married woman with my whole life ahead of me, in front of my grandfather, an aged, widowed man, with nearly all his life behind him. I live because of him. Because of him, my ancestors not only were Napolean and Bessie, Isaac and Eloise, but my heritage stretched back through generations of strong men, to patriarchs named Abraham, Isaac, and Jacob.

While I stood thinking about my physical and spiritual heritage, a nurse came into the room and began to attend to my grandfather. She carried on a one-way conversation with him as she repositioned his body and clothes. I wanted to yell, "Be gentle.

Do you know who this man is? Do you *know* him?" As she cared for him, I wondered if she knew that he, too, had cared for widows and orphans. When she fed him, did she know that he, too, had fed the poor with food, both seen and unseen? When she touched him, did she know that she handled a servant of God? Or was he just another medical chart, another old man, another occupant of a room with a number?

Then, I wondered: Did God look down at Mary two thousand years ago and want to say, "Be gentle. Do you know who this child is? Do you know him?"

Did Mary have similar thoughts when she was in Bethlehem? Did she want to run outside the stable and yell at the top of her lungs that the Son of God had entered the world through her womb? Did she think that gold, frankincense, and myrrh were worthy gifts for her child? Years later, did she have to restrain herself from screaming at those who pierced his side and nailed his hands and feet to a cross, "Do you know him? Do you *know* who this man is? Do you know what he has done, what he is doing for us?"

The true miracle of Christmas is that God, Creator of the universe, the Light of the world, allowed his brilliance to be dulled by the wrap of humanity. Like the fragrant burst of a thousand tangerines against the smell of death was the incarnation of God against a dying world. At the time of his birth, few knew who the child was. But we know. He is Jesus. God in flesh, forever the perfect gift.

three

Surprised by the Unexpected

Ginny Owens has the well-deserved reputation of being a very creative person and a prolific songwriter, it's true (she won the 2000 Dove Award for New Artist of the Year). But few know that she's also esteemed among her friends as a fabulous cook—especially for her hash brown casseroles! During the Christmas season, when she comes off the road to spend time in her home in Franklin, Tennessee, friends congregate in her kitchen for a specially prepared feast and to experience the holiday traditions that Ginny has developed over the years.

An articulate speaker, Ginny chooses words carefully before she answers any questions. Her side of conversations are laced with zinging wit, and friends can occasionally lure her into the famous "Ginny freeze mode"—where she laughs so hard, her blue eyes scrunch up and her face freezes while she makes absolutely no sound at all.

As you will see, twenty-five-year-old Ginny has a decidedly different perspective of Christmas.

GINNY'S STORY

*T*his year I will celebrate Christmas by placing a fresh tree in the living room and decorating my home with angels, nativity scenes, candles, and wreaths. I'll spend a ridiculous amount of time buying and making gifts for friends and family and will host at least one dinner party before the New Year begins. I guess in ordinary circumstances this is fairly predictable holiday activity. Only, my circumstances are not quite ordinary and have not been since I was three. This much is true: I'm an ordinary twenty-five-year-old girl whose life has been made extraordinary by the grace of God.

I guess I could say that, like most people, my life has touches of surprise. I was supposed to be a boy. Everyone, my seminary student father, my school teaching mother, and their doctors in Mississippi, expected a boy. So from the beginning, my family welcomed the unexpected. The next revelation was not nearly as easy to accept. A deteriorating eye condition ran in my family, and even though everyone fervently prayed against my inheriting it, the Lord allowed it, and by my third birthday I was without sight.

My parents were determined that I would grow up as normally and naturally as other children. From the time I could walk, my life was filled with the opportunities sighted children enjoy. We took walks together and stopped to examine blades of grass and petals of flowers along the way. I rode my bicycle around the neighborhood, roller skated, dug the proverbial hole to China in the backyard, and made the neighbors very nervous when I climbed trees all by myself. I proved to be the consummate Christmas tree decorator. There was nothing I couldn't or wouldn't try.

As soon as I was tall enough to climb onto the stool, I discovered the keys of the old piano in the corner of our dining room and began plunking out tunes I heard in Sunday school. My family was full of musical people and someone was always teaching me new songs or singing with me. I remember pounding middle C and E while singing "Jesus Loves Me" and thought it sounded so harmonious!

My family was deeply committed to faith in Christ, so about the same time I discovered music I started learning about the Lord. I was about four when I accepted Jesus as my Savior, and though I didn't know then the depth of meaning behind such a decision, I can see that he has worked in my life and has led me ever since.

Like most children, I was enamored of that wonderful time of year when the air is filled with new songs, new sounds, new smells, and—best of all—new toys! My earliest Christmas memories include the thrilling discoveries of the many different images of the season. As I helped my mother unpack our ornaments and decorations, I examined the handmade angels with haloes, wings, and harps. Round Santas with big hats sat on sleighs pulled by eight tiny reindeer. I loved the nativity scene whittled from wood by my father when he was a boy: shepherds with staves, stable animals, three wisemen, Mary and Joseph, and Baby Jesus in a manger. I lined them up and arranged and rearranged all the pieces in their places. I remember that three large toy camels stood nearby. Since I had never seen any of these objects before, I carefully explored each piece, taking in all the finely crafted details with my fingers. These decorations taught me what Christmas looked like, and their images, even now, are in my mind.

After five or six Christmases had come and gone, my childhood world expanded to include new people and new experiences. I began to learn some of life's hard lessons from people around me. Though I was a bit shy, I was also a precocious child, busy and curious about everything I discovered. Only, it hurt to discover that many sighted people perceived me as "different." I caught their uncertainty when they spoke to me. They hesitated as if my ears didn't work. Maybe even against their own good judgment, they reacted to me not as a normal kid but as a "poor blind child" who couldn't think or act like any other kid her age. For the first time in my life (which hadn't been very long!), I began to sense rejection.

I grew more and more cautious around new people and in unfamiliar situations. I spent more time alone, writing stories and reading books, playing piano and singing. I spent less time riding my bike down the street or exploring undiscovered territories.

Even in this uncertain state, I was still a rambunctious kid with a big mouth and a love for mischief when I felt secure. I liked playing ball, looking for caves, and all the other outside games I played with the neighbor children. Of course, I still loved Christmas and spent months waiting for December to arrive, because it now brought a school vacation as well as the joy of decorating the house, eating sausage balls and gingerbread men, and wrapping gifts.

Throughout my childhood years, I busied myself with school and extracurricular activities like cheerleading, track, and student government. I continued writing music, although I was still very shy about performing it for others. Perhaps this was because I was a timid girl, or maybe it had something to do with the responses I received when I was brave enough to sing in front of people. I didn't often perform, but when I did, I always came away struggling to understand people's strange responses to me. Though I enjoyed communicating with people from stage, I hated those moments right after a performance when a total stranger would pat my shoulder and say, "Bless her heart" before walking away. Often they spoke directly to my mother as if I weren't there, or talked very loudly as if I couldn't hear. Sometimes those occasions caused me to laugh out loud, but mostly I found them humiliating enough that I lost all interest in performing solos.

I grew up attending two schools at the same time—a regular public school and a school for the blind, where I sang in the choir and played in the band. The Christmas programs of my junior high and high school years were especially fun because there were so few of us that I always got several solos and special harmony parts. However, my fondest memory of singing a Christmas solo comes from my senior year of high school. That year, my best friend and I joined the large concert choir at the public high school. Though I was still a shy kid, I thoroughly enjoyed singing with new friends in this 150 member group. I'll never forget my excitement when the choir director chose me as the soloist for "O Holy Night." I was stunned when he called out my name. That was one of those rare but special times when I felt like I had earned something because of my ability rather than being granted it because of my disability. During the concert, I'm sure my voice shook with fear, but the joy of singing that beautiful carol with 150 of my peers was an unbelievably wonderful moment in my life.

As a teenager, Christmas wasn't nearly as thrilling as it had been when I was a younger kid. I still loved the excitement of choosing gifts for my family members but now I loved Christmas because it was a time to reflect on how gracious the Lord was to me and how significant the gift of his Son truly was.

Christmases flew by and almost before I knew it, I was attending college in Nashville, Tennessee. I had a blast studying to become a music teacher. I was so busy with finals and friends that I didn't go home for the holidays until the dorm closed its doors and shooed me away. I was changing and life at home was changing, too. The Christmas tree and all the traditional decorations were up by the time I arrived, but it wasn't the same. I was struck with the realization that as I grew older, so did everyone else! My younger brother was now in high school, my wonderful grandparents were growing frail. My biggest surprise was that life at home continued without me, and I had only a short time at Christmas to catch up on all the latest news.

Back in Nashville, I kept writing music, occasionally performed at college events or in local church services, and pursued my teaching degree. My university was a competitive world and many of the music students were more advanced than I, so opportunities to sing or play were limited. Besides, as I had felt a few years earlier, displays of pity for me were enough to keep my performances to a bare minimum. But at the beginning of my junior year, I had opportunities to lead my college peers in worship, both in informal groups of friends and for organized meetings like Fellowship of Christian Athletes. For the first time ever, I found a way to communicate from stage that was exciting for me both during and after it happened. There isn't anything quite as awesome as hearing a group of people singing praises to Jesus, and realizing that my only responsibility was to worship made it even more meaningful.

I went into my senior year with my future totally laid out in my mind. I would teach junior high or high school choir and piano, write in my spare time, and possibly lead worship in a local church. This seemed like a satisfactory use of the gifts God had given me and of the knowledge I'd acquired over the last four years. Funny, isn't it, how God's plans surprise us with the unexpected, or at least prove quite different from the ones we come up with!

I'll never forget the Christmas holiday of my senior year. I was a nervous wreck. All my courses were completed and I was about to embark upon a semester of student teaching. I would spend eight weeks teaching choir and piano at a large public high school where at least half of my students were from other countries and the rest were from the inner city. After that, I would seek a permanent teaching job. By this time next year, my life would be significantly different. I knew that. Only, I had no clue what that meant. I had no idea! So, as in Christmases before, I concentrated on the knowledge that God sent his Son because of his love for me rather than on my unknown future.

The Lord kept me alive through my first semester of student teaching. I had to learn how to keep the wanderers in their seats and they had to learn how to read my handwriting, but we all had a great time learning together. Armed with actual classroom experience, a teaching license, and a college graduate's resumé, I pounded the pavement, determined to find a job with my name on it. At the same time, I developed a friendship with a man in my church who was a recording engineer in Christian music. After he heard me sing the only solo I'd ever sung at church, he asked a mutual friend if I was a full-time musician. We were introduced and eventually he helped me record a demo of several of my songs at his home studio. He and his wife became good friends, and they both seemed confident that the Lord could use my music in ways I hadn't even considered. This seemed contrary to the opinion of most of my friends who listened to the demo. The general consensus was that my voice was nothing out of the ordinary, which didn't surprise me. I agreed with them.

I continued looking for a teaching job. Principals seemed quite afraid to hire a blind person to teach sighted students. That didn't surprise me, either. However, I was sure that eventually I'd find someone who felt differently and was willing to take a chance. So I kept knocking on doors and the doors remained shut. One day in the middle of the summer, I unenthusiastically answered a phone call. My engineer friend called to say that one of his music publishing buddies had heard my demo and was interested in talking to me. In my recently acquired cynicism, I wondered if he, too, would be scared off by my lack of sight. I was pleasantly surprised. We began to meet on a regular basis and I soon realized he didn't doubt my abilities.

But meeting him didn't alleviate my problem. A fairly big problem. Schools were preparing to open for the fall session and I didn't have a teaching contract. Needing work, I applied for any position I could only to meet with the same old fears from potential employers. I finally landed a full-time administrative assistant job. In my spare time, I wrote music with my new publishing friend.

Then, before I knew it, Christmas arrived. Time to be still and know again that God was God; to concentrate on the knowledge of his gifts to me and relinquish any panic or fear over a lack of knowledge for my future. I didn't have any idea of what was ahead and it took a year before I knew the answer to "Why, Lord? Why no teaching contract?"

Twelve months later, I still had questions but not quite the same ones. It was clear I wasn't going to become a schoolteacher any time soon because now I was a recording artist. The progression from making my first demo to signing my first recording contract blurs in my memory, but I'll never forget the new questions that echoed in my mind. Attending the Christmas party hosted by the head of my record label, Michael W. Smith, I sat in his living room, listening to other artists and Michael himself play and sing worshipful songs of praise. I remember thinking, "Dear Lord, you are awesome beyond what I can even imagine. How did you bring me here? Why?"

More Christmases have come and gone, but those questions still ring in my head. They are my annual Christmas questions. I probably won't know the answers until I get to heaven, but I've found that Christmas is the best day in the year to ask, the best day to reflect on all the good gifts the Lord has given us here on earth. Though they aren't always the gifts we would expect, though we may often be surprised when they arrive, the gifts from God are the ones that are best for us.

four

The Significance of a Birthday
Times Seven

Bobbi McCaughey is quickly recognized on magazine covers and television programs as "the mother of the seven babies." But she is much more than a famous parent of the world's first living septuplets.

During our phone interview, I was impressed by Bobbi's honest answers, her deep, easy laughter, and the tearful stretches of silence when she was overcome with inexpressible love for her four daughters and four sons.

Bobbi and her husband, Kenny, are living examples of the admonition, "Be careful what you pray for—you just might get it." Their initial difficulty in conceiving a child led them to fertility specialists and, eventually, their prayer was answered with the joyous birth of their first child, Mikayla. When they prayed for a second child, the results weren't exactly what they expected.

BOBBI'S STORY

Kenny and I always wanted a big family. Well, I wanted six children and Kenny thought more in the vicinity of two or three. But we had difficulty conceiving and only with the help of a fertility specialist was Mikayla born. We hoped that carrying her had corrected some of my hormonal problems, but after 14 months without a second pregnancy we began thinking, "Well, maybe not."

We went back to our specialist and she suggested I try a low dose of Clomid, a common fertility drug. I only considered that for a minute or so before deciding no. We had tried six rounds of Clomid before and it hadn't worked. One pill each morning for five days, keeping close track of my temperature, monitoring for ovulation, was not something I wanted to do again since Mikayla was conceived after a single course of Metrodin, a hormone that stimulates the ovaries to produce eggs.

So for a second time, for eight days in a row, Kenny gave me an injection of Metrodin. A nurse had shown him how to give the shots when we were trying for Mikayla and he really did a good job. I took exactly the same daily dose of two amps as I had before and prayed that God would once again allow the drug to work. Some have criticized us for our decision, but I never felt we were playing the part of God by taking pills or injections. My irregular cycles made conception impossible and I considered the fertility drugs a corrective step to help my body work naturally, just like insulin or estrogen helps correct imbalances.

Our prayers were answered and the Metrodin worked. Our first ultrasound showed three mature eggs, which is exactly what we saw before Mikayla's conception. Three ripe follicles gave us a good chance of conceiving one child, or possibly even twins. After the insemination, Kenny and I waited twelve suspenseful days before going in for a blood test. Then I had to wait several hours before calling the doctor's office for the results. That's when the nurse told me, "Congratulations! You are pregnant."

I was thrilled and, of course, immediately called Kenny at work to tell him we were pregnant. He, in turn, announced the good news to his entire office. Then I called my sister and my mom, knowing they would be thrilled for us. All along I expected what I had experienced before—one child. Mikayla was going to be a big sister to a baby brother or baby sister. But the doctors already knew better. The level of HCG, the pregnancy hormone, was quite high in my blood test results, so it was assumed I was probably carrying twins. Only they didn't tell me that; they just told me what I had prayed to hear: I was pregnant again.

Eleven days later, an ultrasound showed seven sacs. The doctor felt I could be carrying twins, triplets at the most, and the multiple sacs were just reflections. Kenny and I loved the idea of twins and even thought we could handle triplets. Eight and a half weeks into the pregnancy, I watched as the ultrasound scanned one tiny heartbeat, then another, then another—then another. We were not having twins. We were not having triplets. The doctor, the technician, and I were stunned as we continued to count. Five. Six. Seven. Seven sacs. Seven individual little hearts, beating like tiny metronomes.

This certainly wasn't what I expected and not even what I wanted. I was a little scared, a bit angry, and quite puzzled. I wondered what in the world God had in mind. The next two months were very difficult on our marriage. Kenny and I argued about how we could manage a family of ten. Kenny was really torn, thinking God had given us these seven babies but knowing there was no way he could support eight kids. Our 800-square foot house was *way* too small. We didn't have the money to build on and we definitely couldn't afford to move. Kenny was thinking both literally and practically when he said, "We can't do this." We cried together and struggled to want seven more children. The thought of seven babies at once was just incomprehensible.

We learned that seven surviving children had never been born in the United States, but we didn't know about the rest of the world. Kenny looked for information on the Internet, but the only site about septuplets was a fictitious story about seven sisters. That's when we knew for sure that we were headed into new territory and that our lives would be forever changed!

I went to my ultrasound appointments thinking, "Maybe this week there won't be seven." After one visit, I burst into tears when I told my sister and mom, "There's still seven." I knew what I was feeling was wrong. No matter how many babies there were, Kenny and I were blessed to have them. But at that point, I didn't care. Seven was too many. I couldn't imagine carrying them, let alone raising them. The prospect of seven babies completely overwhelmed me.

Nine and a half weeks into the pregnancy, I transferred from the fertility specialist to a high-risk obstetrician. Kenny, his stepmother, my sister, and mom went with me to my first appointment. The doctor wanted everyone present who was going to help me so they would know what to expect, what my limitations were, and how they could best help. The doctor told me in advance, "This is not going to be a 'We're so glad you're pregnant' visit. This is going to be a realistic picture of what to expect. We'll talk about bed rest, proper nutrition, and the chances of seven fetuses living." That appointment was not designed as a happy visit because she wanted us to face the next six months with our eyes open, without any false ideals. She described our future reality and presented a worse case scenario so if something bad were to happen, it wouldn't come out of the blue and find us unprepared.

At the end of the visit, we all watched the ultrasound screen. I was amazed how the babies had grown in just two weeks. At seven weeks, they were just little peanuts with not much in the way of arms and legs or a head separated from a body. At nine weeks, their little arms and legs were more visible and their heads were very identifiable. They all were there, seven tiny bodies wiggling around, seven hearts pounding in unsynchronized rhythm. That view for me was the changing point. My heart went from, "I don't want all these babies" to "I want *all* of these babies." Kenny needed a little more time to really accept seven, but that day, when he looked at those squirming little individuals, he began to feel a father's sense of protection for them, all of them. He was their father and he wanted them in our lives.

Every week we had a routine ultrasound. One week the technician went back and forth over my stomach, counting aloud to six. She couldn't find the seventh baby. I didn't say anything, but my heart hit the floor as I panicked. I tried to remain calm as one side of my brain said, "They can't find one" while the other side of my brain said, "But you have six doing well." Ultrasounds always started at the bottom with Baby Kenny and then moved up. Two girls were right above Kenny, but this time the technician only saw one. It was maybe ten minutes before she realized the girls were mirroring each other and that she actually was seeing both but didn't realize it. I was so relieved. Of course, when I went home and told Kenny about it, I bawled my eyes out. Those ten frightening minutes left no doubt that each one of those children were important members of our family.

Ever since I was a child I've known that God answers prayer, but not necessarily in the way we want or in the way we expect.

Kenny and I prayed for a baby and God in his infinite wisdom, which we will never fully understand, chose to multiply that prayer times seven. Maybe we'll be in heaven before we know why God gave us seven. We do know there is a reason and that God has a plan for the life of each one of our eight children. Maybe their being so well known will give them a platform God can use. We believe everything can bring glory to God, and that along the way there are lessons for us to learn.

Our experience is really a kind of picture of life in general. Good days and bad days are woven together and can't be separated. That's everyone's experience whether they have ten children or no children. We all feel sorry for ourselves sometimes and think that other people's bad days are nothing compared to our own. But then I think, "No, that's not so. Plenty of people have it much worse. Some couples would give their eyeteeth to have seven kids, and I shouldn't complain about anything."

Until the babies were home, I couldn't have imagined our day-by-day routine. Kenny and I repeat the ending phrase of 1 Corinthians 10:13 often! God will provide a way of escape "that you may be able to bear it." Sometimes "bear it" is about the best way to describe parenthood! One day I think, "You guys, what am I gonna do? I wish you were ten years old and could understand when I tell you to do something. Like when I say, 'Don't play in the toilet,' I mean I don't want you to play in the toilet." Or, "I want you to put your own shoes on because I'm tired of tying a hundred pairs of shoes a day." Then by the next day, they won't fight much at all, there won't be much screaming, and nobody throws food on the floor. That's when I think, "This is what it's about." These are the days I live for, when they're just so cute and so much fun.

Our eight children are no different than any other eight kids, except seven go though the same stages at once. It's all fairly normal. We teach them how to brush their teeth, seven sets, how to share, seven times seven. We read bedtime stories, but it resembles story time at the library rather than one parent on a bed with one child. Extended family dinners with aunts, uncles, and cousins are either here or at my sister's house. Eventually, all eight children will have responsibilities and chores, things they'll be expected to do, like help out around the house and mow the lawn. We joke about their future jobs. Mikayla, who is so generous and considerate, will oversee snacks and entertainment. One day Brandon got the mop out and I said, "Oh, Brandon wants to clean the floor." Maybe that will be his job. Joel likes to play in the dryer, so maybe he'll fold all the clean clothes—a full-time job! Someday, we hope to find a small plot of land to plant a garden, and we'll expect all the kids to help grow vegetables to put in the freezer for the winter.

Right now the babies get a lot of outside attention, but even before their birth we knew not to expect much privacy once the public learned of my pregnancy. It's still fairly easy to cooperate with most of the media requests that come along. People are interested in our experiences and I guess I would be, too, if this were happening to someone else. Kenny and I expect that when Mikayla and the babies are older we'll make decisions in family meetings about how to balance our private and public responsibilities. Hopefully, the conclusions we reach and the choices we make will teach them a good work ethic at a young age.

Kenny and I never forget we have been blessed by the kindness of people who have read about our family or have seen us on television. Thanks to the generosity of others, we moved out of our 800-square foot home and into a large house with lots of room for lots of people, which is great since I love a full house. For Thanksgiving last year, our ten and six from Kenny's family got together. I kept thinking, "Boy, there's not very many people here. We all fit at just two tables." It was wonderful having room for everyone.

As the kids grow older, we'll explain that when they were born we were given a lot of help. We know the truth of Philippians 4:19, "My God shall supply all your need according to His riches in glory by Christ Jesus." We would never have thought seven babies at once, eight children in all, was what we wanted or needed for a complete family, but it's what God gave us. Then, he supplied our daily needs with incredible gifts and support from friends, church members, doctors, even total strangers. We'll teach our children the principle found in Luke 12:48, "To whom much has been given, much will be required" (NRSV). We've set up a foundation to assist families with births of triplets or more, so that our experience as a family will continue to bring glory to God. We'll help other parents learn how to handle the extra demands and multiple expenses of special occasions and holidays.

The babies were just barely two last Christmas and weren't really interested in much, but that will probably change. By next year they'll be old enough to sense our anticipation and to question why we have a tree. Each child has a stocking, but they've been empty for the past three years. I'd like to start the tradition of putting little trinkets, like a toy necklace and bracelet or miniature trucks in them, something appropriate to their age and preferences. Until now, they've received the same gifts, but as they mature and show different interests in different areas we'll try to give them each one special thing. In simple terms, we'll tell them that Christmas is the time to celebrate Jesus' birth and that we give gifts to show our love for each other. We will teach them the tree, the lights, the gifts, the music are just ways to help celebrate Jesus' birth. If any family understands the significance of a birthday, it should be ours! At this point, the birthday of our seven is probably the second most widely known in the world.

Last Christmas, someone observed that Mary was specifically chosen as Jesus' mother and wondered if I identified with her. Being asked to compare myself to the mother of Jesus seemed really presumptuous. To me, Mary must have been incredible. But the more I thought about it, I wondered if she and I didn't feel a lot alike when we got our unexpected news. Her family's reaction to her conception probably wasn't unlike my obstetrician's comment during our first visit: "This isn't a 'we're so glad you're pregnant' response."

I wonder if she was afraid of the task God had given her, if she asked, "Why me?" as I did, carrying seven babies inside me. I think almost any Christian woman who learns that something incredible is about to happen in her ordinary life might doubt her ability to face the challenge, even if she knows God is with her. They will probably have the same reaction I experienced: disbelief, maybe some anger and fear, but, eventually, acceptance.

Kenny and I knew that for us to have a second child brought the risk of multiple births. We knew to expect twins or even triplets. Mary prepared herself to bear God's Son, but I doubt that she expected a donkey ride to Bethlehem just before going into labor or the generous gifts of gold, frankincense, and myrrh from strangers. I doubt that she expected the reality of her Son's life— his eventual death on a cross, his resurrection, his ascension. I do identify with a mother who knew about risk and loved her child enough to endure it. Like Mary, I had my own expectations but no idea of how one pregnancy would change everything. Even now, I think I know how life will turn out with eight children—happy, loud, and crowded. I think our Christmases will be full of laughter and littered with piles of discarded wrapping paper. We'll cook tons of food and even have our own choir when we go Christmas caroling! I pray that our Christmases will be a wonderful time of joy and celebration—but I'm sure they won't be what I expect.

The risk of birth

This is no time for a child to be born,
With the earth betrayed by war & hate
And a nova lighting the sky to warn
That time runs out & the sun burns late.

That was no time for a child to be born,
In a land in the crushing grip of Rome;
Honour & truth were trampled by scorn—
Yet here did the Saviour make his home.

When is the time for love to be born?
The inn is full on the planet earth,
And by greed & pride the sky is torn—
Yet Love still takes the risk of birth.

           —Madeleine L'Engle

five

The Silent Power
of a Nativity Set

Eighteen-year-old Sarah held a violin in her hands the first time I saw her walk onto a stage as a concert mistress of a youth orchestra. At such a young age, she already displayed remarkable elegance and composure. During the next ten years of our friendship, I watched her mature into an incredibly beautiful woman of talent, charm, and a mischievous sense of humor.

Her humor gets her through hectic days as a professional manager, responsible for the scheduling of appearances, concerts, promotional tours, and media events for recording artists in a demanding, fast-paced entertainment industry.

The first time I heard Sarah's life story, I was flabbergasted. How could a woman so well educated and well informed have missed the essence of Christmas? Unfortunately, her story is similar to that of many children in modern American homes: affluent, intellectual, and insulated from the truth of Christmas.

≈≈

SARAH'S STORY

By the time I was eight, my large collection of miniature glass animals spilled off my dresser, lined my play table, and littered my bookshelves. My favorites were a momma kangaroo with her tiny baby, a ladybug with teensy little dots, three calico kittens around spilled milk, and an inch-long brown dachshund. I loved them all.

My older sister was the first to collect miniatures and from the earliest times I remember, I tried to be like her. She was smart and the favorite of all her teachers—and our parents, so it seemed to me. Her perfectly placed miniatures were shiny and pristine, no nicks in the paint, no broken legs. My collection didn't compare to hers. Because I played with mine and carried them on imaginary journeys in my pockets, they were chipped and dull, often missing ears, tails, and noses.

My poor comparison to my sister went well past miniatures. Her hamster lived twelve years. I had four that died in rapid succession. Her blue parakeet did tricks, my green parakeet died because I held it too much. She easily got straight A's on her report card while I struggled for my good grades. She did her weekly chores with such a great attitude that she received an additional dollar. There were weeks I didn't get any allowance, let alone a bonus. But I adored my sister and tried hard to be just like her.

I was about nine when the two of us wandered over to a neighbor's garage sale to look at the stuff set out on the driveway and spread across tables. Next to an old flowered teapot and in the shadow of a toy truck, something small caught my eye. I gently picked up three little people, each less than an inch tall. The man's head was no bigger than a kernel of corn and his tiny hand grasped what looked like a gold candy cane. The lady wore a light blue dress and had a funny yellow circle attached to the back of her head. The baby was sleeping in a box and had an even smaller yellow circle glued to his head. I was immediately drawn to this family, assuming they must be angels because of the gold circles. I purchased them with a nickel and ran home to carefully arrange the three pieces on my windowsill. There they stayed, next to the ladybug, for the remaining years of my childhood. I looked over them every night, gazing at the moon and stars through my window. The presence of my miniature family gave me a warm sense of comfort.

In elementary school I was fascinated by stories of the Greeks and Romans, amazed that there were gods and goddesses for everything. My teacher explained that the Romans believed mythological beings ruled over heaven and hell and were responsible for everything that happened in mortals' lives on earth. I was intrigued by their power and mystery. The only god I heard about at my house was one screamed out by someone really angry or in a lot of pain.

I told my mom what we were learning in school and asked who God was. She said there is no real God, that God was something people created to help explain stuff they can't understand. She told me people need a reason for things they are scared of, like death, so they invent a god to help them, just the way the story of Zeus driving his chariot across the sky explains a sunset. I listened to her explanation and it made sense with what my teacher taught me, but in my heart I believed there was a real God. I knew I was right, but I didn't dare say so out loud.

So, still hoping for a better explanation, I walked into the living room to ask my dad and older sister what they thought. Dad told me that when a person dies, that's the end of life. I shuddered when my sister elaborated, saying the type of coffin determines how quickly worms eat a dead body. Dad said nothing happens after death; there is no heaven, no hell, no nothing. When you die, you die. There is no more. My sister nodded in confident agreement. I was completely puzzled. If what they said was true, then it seemed there was no reason to be alive, to exist. I thought about these things, staring out my window at night, over the heads of my serene little plastic family.

During the next summer vacation, one of my school friends came over to play. Looking at my collection of miniatures, she asked why I still had a nativity set out. Puzzled by her question, I glanced around to see what she was talking about. "Your nativity set," she pointed toward the window. She used a word I had never heard before, but not wanting her to know I didn't understand, I just shrugged.

The next December, when it was time to decorate the Christmas tree and the ornaments were carried into the living room, I excitedly dug through every box to find my favorite decoration. I tossed out stuffed Santas and pushed aside snow globes and boxes of tinsel, looking for what I considered the most beautiful ornament we owned. It was about two-inches tall and a half-inch deep, and shaped like a teepee. It hung by a loop of gold thread glued to the very top. The outside plastic was painted brown with gold glitter pasted to it. The inside bland beige was a backdrop for teensy animals and tiny people all painted different colors. I never thought to ask my parents who the people were or why it was the only piece like it in all of our decorations, but every year I chose a spot right in the center, directly in front, so I could see that lovely ornament every time I looked at the tree.

Winter turned to spring, and one Saturday afternoon a girl-friend and I rode our bikes around our neighborhood. She was so sophisticated and smart, so cool. As we pedaled through the streets, she pummeled me with questions to determine if I was cool enough to hang out with her. "Are you a virgin?" she asked. As a fifth grader, I knew by the tone of her voice that this was an important question. I had no idea what "virgin" meant, so with as much disgust as I could muster, I answered, "No!" I could tell she was shocked at my answer, but that didn't stop her from asking, "Do you French kiss? Have you ever had a hickey?" Her responses made me feel like all my answers were obviously wrong, so when she asked, "Are you a Christian?" I fairly shouted, "Yes, of course!" My mind raced around for answers to questions I didn't understand. Confused and bewildered, and not wanting to look like a total loser, I pedaled ahead.

Other questions without answers rang in my mind that year. I spent a lot of time in the silence of night, wondering why I was on the earth. What was the meaning of life? Each night, I drifted to sleep with a final glance at my comforting little family. I couldn't explain my attachment to these cheap, poorly crafted pieces, but somehow their painted faces portrayed love and happiness. They seemed so—peaceful. When it was time for me to pack for college, I reluctantly left them on my windowsill.

During my freshman year at college, Diane and I became friends. She was one of the most beautiful people I had ever met. It wasn't her physical beauty, but an inner beauty that just magnetized people. She was always quick to laugh and smile. Her self-confidence amazed me. We had so much fun together that we got jobs as clerks in the same store and scheduled our shifts for the same days and hours.

Without fail, every Saturday afternoon Diane invited me to go to church with her the next day. I always accepted her invitation and always promised to join her. But my Saturday night partying kept me snug in bed on Sunday mornings while Diane waited for me to show up on the church steps, sometimes for as long as twenty minutes before she gave up and went inside. On Monday mornings, I apologized for standing her up, then promised with all the sincerity I could muster that I would show up the next week. I never did.

Toward the end of the second semester, Diane invited me to a college retreat. "Oh, I can't afford to go," I hedged. Diane assured me it was free. "I have to work," I resisted. "I found someone to cover your shift," she replied. There were no more excuses. "Okay, okay, when do we leave?" I asked with a forced grin.

I purposely missed the bus. The next time I saw Diane, I began my feeble excuses. She looked at me and said, "Sarah, I really want you to learn about God, but I'm not going to force you. I paid your fee to the retreat and I got someone to take your shift so you could go. You're always welcome to come to my church, but I am not going to ask you again."

First I missed the bus, then I missed the trust and respect of Diane. The next Sunday morning I walked into her church. But not alone. I coerced another girl to join me. Diane greeted us with a surprised smile as we slid into the pew next to her. My mind wandered as the man on the stage talked. I spent most of the hour worrying if I was being good enough, if it was okay I was there, especially since I was dressed so differently than the women seated around me. I didn't even *own* a lace-collared dress that covered up my shins! I tried to pay attention so that the God being talked about would love me, too, but nothing made sense to me and my stomach was growling.

After the service, Diane invited me, my friend, and a friend of hers to lunch. After we finished eating, her friend, Dane, began telling us the story of Jesus. He told us about his birth, his crucifixion, and his resurrection. Looking directly into my eyes, he said, "This is what he did for you, Sarah." Even though it sounds silly now, he poured a mound of catsup into each of his hands and stretched them toward me. "He loved you enough to do this, Sarah. Will you believe in him and accept him as your personal Lord and Savior?"

I was mesmerized. For the first time in my life, I heard my reason for living. Someone thought I was valuable enough to live and die for. Someone loved *me*. Tears filled my eyes. What this guy was saying rang true—this wasn't like the mythological stories my teacher told. This was truer than the gods created to explain things humans can't understand; truer than stories of nothing happening after you die, except that worms eat your body. In my heart, I knew this God, this Jesus, was real.

My thoughts were interrupted by my friend shouting, "This is ridiculous! This is so corny. We're outta here. Let's go, Sarah." We had driven to the restaurant in my car so I knew I had to take her home. But Dane had asked a question I wanted to answer. "Yeah. Yes. I guess so," I said and jumped out of my chair. "I'll talk to you about it later," I called back over my shoulder.

The image of red catsup on Dane's hands and the story he told haunted me. I had to hear more about this Jesus, so I returned to Diane's church that night. Some guest speaker was giving his "testimony"—whatever that meant. He told the same story Dane had told at lunch. Then he asked if anyone wanted to come forward and accept Christ. I couldn't get out of my seat fast enough. My heart was beating so quickly I thought it was going to burst out of my chest. I didn't care what I looked like or what people thought of me. I didn't care what I was wearing. This Jesus was Truth and I wanted to run toward him. Some women met me at the front of the stage and then escorted me to a side room and prayed with me.

I immediately drove half an hour to my parent's home to tell them I had become a Christian. They thought I had joined a cult and said, "Just don't give them your money, dear." I raced back to my dorm to tell my roommates. I couldn't stop talking about what Jesus did for me—for them! People needed to know this. Everyone needed to know that Jesus died for every single person—they just had to believe and accept him! This was such incredible news; I couldn't stop talking about it!

Then I told my older sister. My whole life had been spent striving to be like her. I had followed her to the same university, took the same classes, played the violin because she did, and wore the same style of clothes. As a little girl she wore glasses and braces.

I needed neither but made braces out of tin foil and wrapped them around my straight teeth. I had stood in her shadow, believing she was the "good" one. But once I accepted Christ, I became my own person. I no longer needed to be like my amazing sister. I wanted to be me. I really wanted to be like the loving, giving, tender Christ I had just met and as happy as the people who loved him.

When I went home for Christmas break, I walked into my childhood room and my eyes flew to the little family in the window. I picked them up with the new knowledge that they each had a name: The mommy's name was Mary, the daddy's name was Joseph, and the baby's name was Jesus. This contented family was God's family. These little figures that for years radiated love and security to me were, I now knew, a nativity set. This family that watched over me while I contemplated the meaning of life and wondered why I was born, answered my questions.

Now when I'm asked if I'm a Christian, I can say "Yes!" and know with certainty what that means. I knew about Greek and Roman gods when I was a child, but never of a God who loved me personally. My parents are both university professors and they loved me and my brother and sister. They intended to give all three of us an upbringing free of religious bias, unencumbered by childish myths and legends. They intended for us to grow up and make religious associations based on knowledge and fact, rather than superstition or tradition. But what they actually gave us was an empty view of life.

Now going home for Christmas is rather sad. The disposition of our house seems so dark. It's too much hassle for my mom to put up a tree, so she just hangs a cloth "Bah humbug" banner on the brick chimney where we once hung our stockings. When my sister comes home, I see a stark contrast between us. Even with her multiple doctorates, her astounding intellect, her achievements and social status, she doesn't seem content. I irritate her, she thinks I'm too happy; I smile and laugh too much, she says. If I mention God or why Christmas exists, she turns the conversation into an intellectual debate. Faith is not part of her vocabulary.

Every December, when I drive by houses and see decorated Christmas trees shimmering behind glass windows and lighted nativity scenes in front yards, I wonder if children living inside hang ornaments from golden threads without knowing what they represent. I wonder how many children in my own neighborhood look at a nativity set without knowing the names of the mommy, the daddy, and the baby. I wonder how many little girls look through their bedroom windows and contemplate why they were born, why they are here on earth. I wonder how many children celebrate Christmas without knowing the God whose birthday it is; without knowing that the answer to their questions can be found right in their own house—lying in a manger.

Not Just on Christmas Day

The name Leigh Nash may not cause an immediate association with the band Sixpence None the Richer. Her voice, however, is immediately recognized on "Kiss Me," the band's international hit song featured on radio and several movie and television sound tracks. Everyone who knows Leigh and hears the mention of her name says the same thing, "She's one of my favorite people."

Growing up in Texas, Leigh never dreamed she would one day sit in a chair next to David Letterman's desk on *The Late Show*. She was not just the speaker for the band that night, she was a representative of Jesus, the one who calls us to be salt and light in the world.

As Leigh and I talked about childhood Christmases, her sweet disposition took on a slight nervousness unusual in a person accustomed to being on the stage. Listening to her unfolding story, I understood. Life has not allowed her the luxury of naiveté, but godly choices have produced in her an innocent and pure spirit. Leigh's faith is the foundation for her life, both in and out of the spotlight.

LEIGH'S STORY

My first Christmas memories are of me with my sister, Molly, opening gifts at our grandmothers' houses. We'd go from one grandmother's to our other grandmother's to open even more gifts. Believe me, we had gifts *galore*! Our early childhoods were filled with lots of love, lots of attention, and plenty of comfort. As far as we knew, life was secure and predictable. Later, we had to face a reality that would change our opinion and change us forever.

Just as my sister and I were beginning our lives, our father, a young banker with a bright future, turned onto a very long road of alcoholism. His wayward journey made my mom launch a massive campaign to keep Molly and me from knowing too much. She meant to protect us from our dad's binges and carelessness. More than anything in the world, Dad loved us, but he was very divided, as though he had two different personalities. One was a loving and devoted husband and father; one was a loose cannon who made weird friends everywhere he went. Once he started drinking, there was no finding the stop button.

Dad had a knack of befriending people with shady pasts and dubious futures. He seemed drawn to the periphery of society. His generosity and goodness countered a wild side where he pretty much flew by the seat of his pants. My mother, on the other hand, grew more calm and stable, determined that my sister and I would be unaffected by my dad's behavior. She had a "Father Knows Best" fantasy playing in her head, intensified by a strong sense of pride. She was obsessed with hiding Dad's problem and protecting his reputation among his peers and employers. We all know now how impossible this was. Like most enablers, she tried to take full responsibility for two babies and our dad.

Mom and Dad were actually a pretty good match and they loved each other dearly. When he wasn't drinking, Dad was always fun. His quick wit and quirky sense of humor made us all laugh. Saturday mornings were great. The four of us rode bikes, had picnics, and planned what we would do when one of Dad's big business deals came through. For all his weaknesses, Dad is the one who taught us to dream.

My father wasn't abusive when he drank but he was completely undependable. He couldn't be counted on to be home when he said he would. When he did arrive, we never knew which dad he would be—the loving, supportive dad, the silly teenager, or the angry, bitter man who smelled of alcohol. Mom constantly worried about his choice of friends and his inability to stop drinking once he started. And though she tried, she couldn't keep Molly and me from a constant state of uncertainty.

When Molly was ten and I was eight, my father shocked us all with the decision to quit his job at the bank. He always wanted to be an entrepreneur and his passion for new business ventures quickly destroyed the remaining façade of being a normal family. Now, on top of his drinking, family finances became a major source of tension and arguments. We paid a very dear price for my dad's entrepreneurial spirit.

First, my father invested all our money into his endeavors, and, not surprisingly, for a long time brought in very little income. My mother returned to work as a schoolteacher, and we moved from the nice house we had grown up in and settled into a small apartment in a different part of town, a real pride-swallowing event for us. It was obvious to our friends that we took a step down, but Mom assured us we were learning a good lesson in humility. She said this was building our character and that we were going to be better people for it.

Mom wouldn't rely on Dad for normal parental-type stuff. She couldn't really. She was a little overprotective and limited his input in our lives, with good reason. If we knew Dad was supposed to pick us up from school, Molly and I were on edge all day. I didn't invite friends over because I never knew if he would show up with liquor on his breath and act completely crazy. My friends might not have noticed, but I would know right away. It was so embarrassing when he said silly things or acted like a wild adolescent. I realize now that my nervous disposition and anxiousness started pretty early and my mom's attempts to hide the truth behind artificial smiles only frightened me more.

All this time, we attended church. My dad carried the collection plate for offerings and for a while taught a first-grade Sunday school class with my mom. Eventually, he stopped going to church because he was embarrassed by the difference between his success as a banker and the lack of it as a businessman. He felt people were judging him and he didn't want to face their barrage of questions. He actually started to feel bitter about the "perfect people" at our church. I guess that's not too unusual. He was hurting and couldn't relate to anyone who seemed to have it all together. But Dad never lost his passion for his new business; he wasn't about to stop pursuing his dream. He always believed that success was just around the corner and when it arrived, he would become the husband and father he wanted to be.

We had an incredible amount of debt to pay off while we lived in the apartment. My parents argued a lot about it while my mom paid bills with her teaching income. In spite of our financial crisis, Molly and I didn't worry about food or clothes, we worried when our parents fought. We didn't know what was going to happen between them. We knew they loved each other, but their relationship was tumultuous. A lot of fights happened late at night. They never physically abused each other, but they yelled a lot and threatened to leave, which scared Molly and me really badly. My sister tried to protect me during these sessions, telling me to go back to bed, but I just snuggled next to her at the banister, held onto the railings, and listened. When things got really unbearable, we would run downstairs to mediate.

Big fights always turned into family counseling sessions with my dad. The three of us cried and told him, "You're really blessed. We love you and we're sticking with you. Why are you so selfish about this business? Why do you drink and hang out with these people?" There were countless conversations like that, the three of us trying to make things better.

Things didn't get better. One Christmas, I remember going to the mall to window-shop. Mom stood in front of a Christmas store and just wept. Molly and I felt horrible and wondered if we had done something wrong. All my mother wanted growing up was a wonderful storybook family, and we couldn't make that happen. Looking through the store window at other families buying new decorations and ornaments for their homes made Mom realize just how bad things were for us. She thought, "Why can't we have that? Why can't things be like that for my girls?" It made her incredibly sad and then she felt even worse for crying in front of us.

That year, Christmas Day was no better, either. A long-standing feud between my father and my mother's mother meant Dad stayed home while we went to Grandmother's house. She didn't understand why my mom stayed with my dad. For years, Mom's entire family encouraged her to leave him, but Mom wanted to honor her marriage. She prayed about their relationship and felt leaving Dad wasn't the right thing to do.

So Mom, Molly, and I spent half of Christmas Day at my grandmother's house and the other half of the day at home watching movies and snacking with Dad. It was kind of lame, to be honest. We tried to be strong, especially Molly. If I ever complained, she told me not to be selfish, not to let my mom see my discontent. She seemed to have a better understanding and maturity than me.

Our early Christmases with lots of gifts became Christmases with gifts that only put us deeper in debt. Then those few gifts dwindled down to no gifts, except those from our grandmother. After Dad left the bank, and for as long as she could, Mom scraped enough money together to keep Christmas fun. We probably could have sold stuff to get cash if we really wanted to, but we agreed that was more trouble than it was worth. In our hearts we understood that gifts were unimportant but with the cultural influence of commercialism, we had a hard time acting on that knowledge. We did some cool things though. When we did give gifts, Mom insisted that each one have a short poem attached that hinted of the item inside. Some of those verses are stuffed in a drawer at home—they're so much fun to read now!

My mom believed that the birth of Jesus was the reason for everything, and she tried to make us all see that, but without our support her effort turned into a disaster. We sat impatiently while she read the Christmas story from the New Testament and then we'd hang out all day, watching movies with Dad. We tried to pretend that it didn't matter if we didn't receive any gifts. We tried to focus on the fact that we were together, we were safe, and we had a roof over our heads. We had clothes to wear and food to eat.

As my high school years went by, I learned so much about how the lack of material things affects perceptions, about being humble, about knowing what's important in life, and how to love. I learned that, even though we try, we humans can't love unconditionally. I learned a lot about grace and forgiving people we love. Those are pretty important lessons to grasp so young, and I'm really thankful for them. I don't think I would take back any of those unusual Christmases.

Another major event occurred in our family's life after I graduated from high school and went on the road with a band. My parents separated for almost four years. Each of them suffered their own version of hell on earth during that time. There was no more fighting, but a lot of time for contemplation, change, repentance, and, finally, forgiveness. After much personal soul-searching, they are back together, healing what was once a disastrous marriage. They lived through so much together, and overcoming the pain of their past is a constant reminder of God's grace to them. Their reconciled marriage is a miracle, really. There are no secrets between them and they share everything. This is such a good example for Molly's marriage and for mine.

I cannot imagine why I am so blessed. My husband is amazing, and I have a great career. I used to wonder how my parents managed to raise two good, levelheaded daughters, because alcoholism is definitely a family disease. I know now it had everything to do with God. I believe he has a special place for families who try to keep him at the center, even though they're messed up and weak and hurting. God showed my family so much grace by taking such good care of us.

After years of silence between my dad and my grandmother, he went to her house and apologized for his behavior. My grandmother forgave him and they mended fences. It was a huge step for both of them. My father understood she was just being protective of her daughter and grandchildren, and I think she understood his new sincerity.

And then Dad apologized to my sister and me. For years we warned him, "You're going to be so sad when we're grown and out of the house and you don't have us anymore. Someday you'll be sorry that you chose this business over us." None of us knew how intense that sorrow would prove to be. Fortunately, we've been given time to repair our relationships. We've cried a lot together, and we've assured Dad that we always loved him. Still, I can only imagine the feelings he has over what "might have been."

To this day, our Christmases are not very traditional. We still don't give gifts at my parents' house. They have a tree and adequate financial resources, but it's just not our tradition at all. We spend the morning reflecting on what Christmas is all about. And now we finally listen when the Scripture is read! We still like to watch movies with Dad, so usually we all go see whatever's released that day. It's just our way to spend Christmas together.

My husband and I alternate Christmases between his parents and my parents. At his parents' house, it's like Gift Central with piles of presents for all the grandkids. I get a little bit misty-eyed seeing the kids run and laugh and tear into gifts. I wish I could go back and give that to my mom. She didn't get enough of that with Molly and me. She seldom felt sure that her daughters were really happy. She wanted to spoil us some, like most mothers do, especially when she knew she couldn't.

We didn't really miss a lot. We received gifts that will last a lifetime. Mom showed us what it means to be faithful. She taught us how to keep our dignity when the judging eyes of those around made our home a fishbowl. She modeled commitment and the willingness to grow. She sang beside us in church with her head held high and her eyes focused on God's promises.

Dad showed us the consequence of what happens when career becomes more important than family. Then, he showed us humility and the intensity of love and just how much a life can change when touched by God's forgiveness and grace.

I learned about pride from both my parents. Pride can either uphold you or destroy you and, in any case, it had better be given to God for his use. Mom and Dad modeled true love. They held on to each other, rich or poor, healthy or sick, better or worse, together or apart. They never gave up on their marriage or each other. Now they amaze me. They hold hands in church and just glow with happiness and contentment. Seeing them this way is a gift I never imagined having. It's so much more special because God is obviously with them.

As I look back, I realize that through the good and bad I lacked for nothing. God gave us proof that he does supply all our needs. Without presents on Christmas Day, we learned to focus entirely on God's gift, a Savior to love us, accept us, and forgive us. Love was the important gift we had every year. The assurance of love. The promise of love. The expression of love. Our difficult experiences gave us great empathy and awareness of other people's pain. We know now to listen and to relate to people who experience humiliation, anxiety, or worry. Love and compassion are the gifts that were given to us and the ones we give to others. And not just on Christmas Day.

seven

Perfect Gifts Are Possible

Da'dra Crawford Greathouse is acclaimed as "one of the greatest voices in Christian music." As a member of the recording group Anointed, she has rightfully received numerous Dove and Stellar Awards, as well as Grammy and Nammy nominations.

When I met Da'dra in her home, she was a picture of relaxation: makeup-free and comfortably dressed in baggy sweats and a T-shirt. We laughed about the difference between our private and public appearances! Her serenity was quite a contrast to the energetic spirit of her performance persona.

When Da'dra performs, she bounds onto the stage like she owns it, holding nothing back, commanding the attention of the audience. Her passionate and authoritative rendition of a song brings enthralled crowds to their feet, applauding not only her talent, but her Lord. General consensus is: "Now that girl can sing!" Both on and offstage, Da'dra radiates a joy and contentment she did not always feel.

Da'dra's Story

Two Christmases in my life stand out. One was the happiest of my life and one was the saddest. The saddest was the Christmas I was twelve. A couple of months earlier, Mom surprised my two younger brothers and me with a puppy, a hyper little ball of beige fluff. My parents had divorced the year before and I think she was trying to bring some happiness and distraction into the house. It worked. My brothers and I instantly loved the puppy's cute nose, floppy ears, and round brown eyes. His size was mini but we named him Maxie.

Early that Christmas morning, Mom, Steve, Brian, and I crowded around the tree opening gifts. "Maxie," we called. "Maxie, time to open your presents." Plastic bones and puppy toys childishly wrapped for him were under the tree. "Come on, Maxie," we called, expecting him to bounce into the room yapping and jumping and licking our faces. But he didn't come and the silence was eerie. Steve got up to search. "Maxie!" he called. His voice pitched up. "Maxie?" He looked under the table, behind the sofa. He searched our bedrooms and the kitchen; he even went downstairs and scanned the basement. No Maxie.

We all joined the search, a quartet of voices calling Maxie's name. When Mom suggested we try the basement again, the three of us followed right on her heels. Halfway down the stairs, we saw Maxie's leash looped around a step. We forced our eyes to follow the length of blue plastic rope. None of us was prepared for the sight of our puppy dangling from the end of his leash. It was awful and we cried out in horror. Obviously, he tried to climb the stairs but slipped and fell between two of them. The leash caught around a step, hanging our precious Maxie.

I remember taking on the role of big sister, helping Mom comfort Steve and Brian. I tried to assure them that Maxie's death was no one's fault. I explained that they weren't responsible, that things happen we can't control. I could say it about our puppy, but I couldn't make myself believe it about our father leaving us. I felt it was my fault, like most children who blame themselves for their parents' separation. Tears still on our faces, we went to the kitchen, our special gathering place.

Mom was the anchor of our family and over the years we spent a lot of time in the kitchen with her. It was the place we laughed, the place we talked, the place we sang. Almost daily, while Mom cooked, we did our homework, told our stories, squabbled, and received our reprimands. We were comforted by the presence of Mom and by the aroma of steaming vegetables and roasting chicken, baking pies and melting cheese. And never more so than on Christmas Day.

Mom was a professional cook for nineteen years and when she prepared Christmas Dinner...oooh, it was a feast! Ham, turkey, baked beans, greens, sweet potatoes, candied yams, macaroni and cheese, the works! Rolls, sweet potato pie, pineapple upside-down cake. It was all so delicious, I often went back for seconds—no wonder I was always struggling with weight!

The Christmas before losing Maxie was our first year without Dad at home. Our parents had separated a few months before and we were having a hard time adjusting. I was a child and didn't realize just how much Mom was affected. That year, when my brothers and I got up on Christmas morning, we found Mom sitting in a kitchen chair. We thought she was just taking a break from cooking, but she was crying. Mom never cried in front of us, *ever*, so we knew something was really wrong.

I remember our asking, "Mom, what is it? Mom? Mom, please, *please* tell us what's wrong." Tears streamed down her face and I wondered if she needed to go to the hospital or something. Then, in a choked voice, barely above a whisper, she said, "I'm sorry. I just wish I had more to give."

The three of us kids had heard words like *divorce* and *child support*, but we didn't know a whole lot about what they meant. We didn't have a clue about the word *repercussions* until we glanced around the kitchen. There weren't nearly as many big pots on the stove as usual. I didn't see a turkey thawing or a cake cooling. The counters weren't cluttered with dirty cutting boards, batches of mixing bowls, or stacks of sticky pans. Something was wrong, for sure.

Mom's shoulders trembled as she cried, "I didn't have enough money for lots of presents or toys...there's only a ham and greens," she sobbed, "no pie." The realization of what she was saying dawned upon me. I looked helplessly at Steve and Brian and then back at our mother as she blurted out, "You deserve so much more...you're such *good* kids."

Being the oldest, I felt like I needed to say something, *anything*, to comfort her and let her know we were all right. I remember my honest words as if I spoke them yesterday. "Mom, look at it this way, we get to lose weight." It worked. She started to laugh. Then Steve chimed in. "Yeah, Mom, look at it that way." That made us laugh all the harder, coming from my skinny-as-a-stick brother, so serious with his bony arms and legs.

I meant what I said about losing weight. But I didn't lose weight that Christmas, or any other Christmas. There's a picture that shows my folded arms resting on top of my extended tummy. That's how big I was. Even in kindergarten, kids called me names and made fun of me, and in elementary school I was always the last one picked for sports and games. I wanted to fit in so badly, to have more friends, to hang out with the popular, thin girls with the long, beautiful hair. I was convinced that my being overweight had something to do with my father not wanting to stay at home. Instead of giving me feminine gifts for my birthday or for Christmas, like a necklace or a pretty dress to wear to church, he gave me a jump rope and a Tummy Toner. He meant well, and I knew he loved me, but I was on the verge of my teen years, feeling ugly and critical of myself. I was sure no one liked me, and I didn't like me either. I spent a lot of time alone in my room, doing homework, listening to music on my headphones, lying on my bed, crying in my pillow so that no one would hear me.

I had one close friend: Jesus. And I talked to him a lot. I started getting up an hour early before school so I could pray. After school in the afternoon, when my brothers watched TV, I'd go to my room to pray. Not only was I a "fat pig" and unappealing because of the way I looked, no one wanted to hang out with me because I was a spiritual freak. I guess not too many twelve years olds read the Bible and prayed so much. But maybe not too many felt as desperate.

Adolescence is a pretty horrible time for most kids, even under the best conditions, and I was no exception. My life seemed overwhelming. My dad had left, Maxie had died, and I didn't have many friends. I was always an honor roll student, but by age thirteen, my appetite increased and my grades dropped. I constantly thought of ways to take my own life.

One day after school, I decided to slit my wrists. I went into the kitchen and looked at my mom's collection of professional cutlery—there was a vast selection to choose from. Still deciding, I heard the phone ring. I knew it would be Mom calling to make sure I was home. I always arrived first and then took care of Brian and Steve for a few hours until Mom got in from work. It didn't occur to me how horrible it would be for my brothers to find me if I went through with my plan. I answered the phone.

"Hello." I expected Mom's voice but no one responded. "Hello?" I asked again. No answer. I hung up. It was time to make my choice. Just as I reached out for a knife, the phone rang again. "Hello?" Nobody on the line. "Hellloooo?!" I hung up. "Oh, well. I'm gonna do it this time," I thought. The phone rang again. "Hello!" Silence. No one was there. I slammed the phone down, back into the receiver. Three times the phone had rung. Three times no one spoke. I was puzzled; that had never happened to me before. Then I remembered: Three times God called out to young Samuel to get his attention. Eli, the prophet, instructed Samuel, "If he calls you, say, 'Speak Lord, for I am listening.' "

I began to cry. If God was trying to get my attention, he got it. Only, instead of asking the Lord to speak to me, I began to speak to him. All my tears and complaints poured out. I was so hurt by the name-calling and teasing. I hated being a fat girl and ugly. I admitted how angry and afraid I was since my father left, how confused and lonely I felt. I asked God to forgive me for even considering taking my own life. Finally, completely cried out, I sat in silence and felt the comfort and love of God surround me. Then I heard God speak to me: "I have a great plan for your life."

I didn't know exactly what it was, but I knew it meant I had a reason to live and had a new start. Not much seemed to change the next day, but I knew everything had changed. I still didn't have many friends; I still considered Jesus my best friend and didn't let a day go by without reading the Bible. I even took it to school with me. I memorized scriptures and prayed "without ceasing."

My mom noticed I spent a lot of time praying and reading my Bible, and she saved money for my next Christmas gifts, two gifts that changed the direction of my life: a King James Version Hebrew/Greek Key Study Bible and the new live album by the Hawkins Family. I still have that Bible. It's beat up, the cover is worn, the pages are tattered, and verses are underlined, but it's my favorite Bible of all time. I listened to that Hawkins Family record over and over and fell in love with gospel music. Who I am today started that

Christmas with two sensitive gifts from my mother. I couldn't see it then, but that's when the long process of my healing began.

When I started high school, I was still a chubby little girl. I threw myself into academics to keep busy and as a way to avoid the people avoiding me. I finished my freshman year with a 3.9 GPA. I closed my sophomore year with a 3.8. On a whim, I challenged myself to make straight A's during my junior year and did. I also did something else. I stopped eating. I began exercising as religiously as I prayed. I lost weight, a lot of weight. Naturally, my mom noticed. She cooked fabulous dinners that I refused by saying, "I'm not hungry," which was usually not true, or "I'm fasting," which was sometimes true since I fasted and prayed on Wednesdays for spiritual growth. The other six days, I ate very little or not at all so I could lose weight.

I entered my last year of high school thinner and with a GPA higher than anyone else's in the senior class. I was named Valedictorian, the first African-American in the school's history to earn that title. But instead of being happy and proud, I felt apologetic. My physics teacher, who was always tough on me, thought someone else deserved the honor, a very beautiful girl. I was devastated. I lost weight, but still perceived myself as fat. I had achieved my academic goals, but felt like a failure. I won honors, and yet the negative opinion of one person was enough to crush my self-esteem. I let the perceptions of others shape my perception of myself.

My response was more self-control and greater demands for achievement. No matter what I tried, I went for it with gusto! I gave life my all, and I still do. Only then, I was criticized for being too dramatic, too deep, too smart, or too spiritual. Those words hurt. But it hurt the most when I was criticized for my faith. I loved God wholeheartedly and even that drew flak. I felt as though everything about me was commented on by someone—every talent, achievement, attitude, and even my devotion.

Even my singing wasn't exempt from public opinion. I never really thought I was a great vocalist, but I became convinced of that by people's comparison to my brother, Steve. "Girl, your brother, ooh-ooh, now he can *sing!*" My greatest joy was singing with my brother—he *is* good! We sang together all our lives and loved the way our voices blended. I sang alto and Steve sang soprano—well, until his voice changed! We had so much fun rehearsing together, but eventually the thrill of singing with him was deflated by well-meant but insensitive questions. "What are you going to do when your brother grows up and makes it big in music?" I understood the clear implication: "He is *definitely* the more gifted of the two of you."

I was always compared to my brothers. Adult friends or members of our church would just go on and on about Steve and Brian's gorgeous, round, hazel-green eyes and long, curly eyelashes. Even total strangers would gush to Mom, "Goodness, their eyes are so beautiful!" Then they'd turn to me, appraise my plump body and plain brown eyes, and murmur in a flat voice, "Oh, is this your daughter?"

Even people who should have known better wounded me with their words. I'll never forget one particular minister's counsel: "Da'dra," he began, "I really don't think you 'have it' like your brother Steve." I really didn't hear much more after that, just enough to hear him say I should pursue academic options. He directed me away from singing and toward other areas of ministry, like teaching or evangelism. I really laugh now, because I do both those things—in song!

I followed that minister's advice by continuing my education. I went off to college looking trim and curvaceous and managed to fulfill a childhood dream: I was popular. Moving into my dorm room the weekend before classes started, some guys on campus came by to ask my name and get my phone number. It was pretty overwhelming, really. I went from no dates in high school to being one of the most sought-after girls in college. But I found the dynamics of dating completely stressful. It sounds strange, but every guy I dated wanted to marry me. Before I finally decided, "Enough!", I had fallen in love and accepted a proposal. But that engagement was quickly broken when my fiancé announced we were getting married—soon. I was hesitant and he wasn't. "I am getting married this year," he vowed, "with or without you." He did. Without me.

The adjustment to the newness of college life was hard and, like most freshmen, my grades dropped. I was the first in my family ever to attend college and after my first semester I was put on academic probation. The straight A's I had made in high school without much effort didn't prepare me for the fast college pace. Plus I missed my family and they missed me. It took a while, but by my sophomore year, the old gusto was back. I made the Dean's list and remained there until graduation. It helped when I decided to avoid serious relationships with men. Dating was fine, but after falling in love a time or two, I realized it was too distracting and hurt too much. I still dated a lot, but I kept my guard up and let every guy know, in no uncertain terms, that I was only interested in friendship. I was in control.

Then I met Mark. He was the new youth pastor at my church and I was a singer in the praise and worship team. One Wednesday night, our pastor introduced this new guy to the congregation before asking him to pray. Mark was just a few words into his prayer when his voice and words caught my attention. My eyes flew open and I stared at him. "Who is this guy?" I thought. "What a godly man." I liked his spirit. Something about him was special. I checked him out for a while after that and never saw him with any girl. I tried to flirt with him, but he just smiled, quietly asked, "How are you?" and then before I could say another word, he walked away with a "God bless you." I was intrigued. Later I found out that he asked my mom for permission to date me, but never got around to asking *me*. Actually, I had to ask him.

It was my senior year of college at Capital University, and I was being honored along with other top students around the country who participated in the Minority Scholarship Program. Ohio State University hosted this annual event so students could check out their graduate program. The Winans always gave a concert that weekend, and I heard that Mark was singing in one of the opening groups. I casually said to him, "Hey, wait a minute. You're singing there? Well, I'm gonna be there, too, so why don't we go together?" That's how it began and five years later we were married.

All this should have made me happy: my graduation from college with honors, falling in love with a wonderful man, my marriage, and an incredibly blessed career singing in Anointed with my brother Steve and close friend Nee-C. But I wasn't happy and the problem was me.

Even after a few years of marriage, I was convinced Mark deserved someone with confidence, someone beautiful, not someone insecure like me. I put my husband through a lot. He loved telling me, "You are so beautiful." But I'd brush if off, saying, "No, I'm not" or "What are you talking about?" Finally, it got to the point where I'd say, "Stop telling me that. It's not true." At first, he thought I was being modest or overly humble. I thought he was just trying to be sweet. But the more he said it, the more agitated and irritated I became. Before long, my childhood feelings of ugliness resurfaced and my lack of self-esteem became an issue in our marriage.

Mark wondered how I could think so poorly of myself. After a long day on a video shoot, I was able to give him a perfect reason. We were making an Anointed video when the cameraman stopped the filming and yelled, "Do something about her arms." My arms. He was talking about mine, partially exposed in a short-sleeved T-shirt. Makeup and wardrobe people came running over to conceal the limbs he found so offensive. I was humiliated even more when I heard him mutter, "Why can't the other girl sing the solo on this song? I could shoot her better."

I blurted out the horrors of the day to Mark. He gently held me and said, "You are beautiful, my lady. But I'm not going to beat you over the head with this anymore. I'm just going to pray; pray that God will help you see how beautiful you really are. I can tell you until I'm blue in the face and you won't believe me. So I'm going to pray for you."

Mark was very serious, very gentle, and I was very afraid. I was afraid that he would leave me. Afraid he would abandon me because I wasn't thin or beautiful. But Mark was right. Only prayer and God could change me or cause me to see Mark's love for me.

"God, help me," I pleaded, "help me see myself differently." Every time I saw my reflection, I asked to see a beautiful person rather than an ugly one. I wanted beauty on the inside *and* the outside. I didn't want just an exterior "makeover." I wanted beauty to come from the development of my character.

Every morning, I got up, looked in the mirror and said, "You are beautiful. God loves you." I didn't mean it, but I said it. I hoped if I said it every day, maybe I'd believe it. Then one day, as I gazed into the reflection of my face and watched the tears roll down my face, I believed it. Revelation, like a light, came on. God made me. God made *me*. He created me the way I am. If I hated myself, I insulted his work and wisdom. I realized, looking at myself in the mirror, that when God looks at me, he responds as he did when he first looked at all of creation: "This is good. *Very* good."

On the Christmas Day we lost our puppy, Maxie, I told my brothers we shouldn't blame ourselves for things we can't control. I understand that better now. I can't control the genetic shape of my arms or the color of my eyes. I can't control the center of my voice or my height. But some things can be controlled and some things can be changed. I can take care of my health and appearance. I can work out to keep my arms from getting flabby. I can improve my voice by using it regularly and wisely. I can polish the gifts God gave me. I can prioritize events and demands that come my way. It's a waste of precious time to sit around worrying how I look, whether I'm collecting awards, whether an audience applauds louder for some other artist over Anointed. My goals are to become a godly woman, to please God, be a loving, healthy wife, and, someday, a good mom.

A Christmas picture from last year shows me with my folded arms resting on top of my extended tummy, proof that I am big again. But this time I'm happy, and, as they say, great with child. My rounded belly is a haven for our baby. When the photo was taken, I was resting on the couch with my eyes closed. I remember the warmth from the logs burning in the fireplace and the fragrance of pine from our decorated tree. I was so content, so at home. After the camera flashed that silent night, I looked over at my husband and caught him smiling at me. Christmas lights reflected off the tears in his eyes.

"What?" I asked him. "You are so beautiful," he whispered. "I know," I smiled. "Merry Christmas."

Evan Christopher entered this world weighing 6 pounds, 12 ounces, with a towering stature of 19 1/2 inches. Mother and child are doing well.

The soul,
who is lifted by a very great and yearning desire
for the honor of God and the salvation of souls,
begins by exercising herself for a certain space of time in the ordinary virtues,
remaining in the cell of self-knowledge,
in order to know better the goodness of God towards her.

This she does because knowledge must precede love,
and only when she has attained love
can she strive to follow and to clothe herself with truth.

—Catherine of Siena
The Dialogue

eight

The Christmas of
Second Chances

Carolyn, mother of three teenagers—two daughters and a son squeezed in between—is not what most of us would call a typical pastor's wife. She can get more done than nearly anyone I know, but manages to do it all about five minutes late. Most of her day is spent driving kids to whatever sport is in season, pulling smelly uniforms and half-eaten fast food meals from beneath car seats, and filling the lives of her church family with brightness.

She considers herself an approachable extrovert. Without a doubt she's a fun-loving woman and may never outlive being teased for wearing two different shoes in public—which she's done more than once! Many women consider her a good friend, a confidant and comforter, and a woman of prayer, a nurturer with a listening ear.

Expectations of pastors' families always run high, but through years of experience Carolyn has learned to simplify the holidays and find balance between her commitments to Christ, family, and the demands of service.

CAROLYN'S STORY

By the time I was twenty-three, Mark and I had met, married, and started our first church. We each had grown up assuming parental duties in our families, still it seemed a little ridiculous to be a senior pastor's wife at age twenty-three. Mark was only twenty-six, so it was a quick maturing experience for both of us.

We didn't intend to start our work in the ministry as "Senior Pastor." Mark and I had been sent by our denomination to help six couples begin a new church. They excitedly told everybody they knew about our plans, and by the time the "real" pastor showed up, we all loved each other so much we couldn't imagine a change. With gratitude to the way the Lord works, the "real" pastor didn't stay but we did. At our very first official service in the local high school, Mark preached to a congregation of over 350 people. We were on our way!

In November of that year, our first child was born. Mark and I were proud parents when she was chosen to play the role of Baby Jesus in the church's first Christmas program. Because of her, in our eyes, it was a very human, very realistic production. Only, just as the demure, sixth-grade Virgin Mary stood up, little "Baby Jesus" wet all down the front of her costume. Poor suffering Mary stood totally drenched, holding a wet, relieved, and happy holy infant. What a way to introduce the pastor's family to the community! Maybe then I should have realized we would never be a typical household.

Undaunted by our child's start and my own lack of experience, I wanted to establish wonderful Christmas traditions for our growing family. It wasn't as easy as I expected. We started with a lovely fresh tree and our daughter's eyes were swollen shut by the time we realized she was allergic to pine. Out went the fragrant real tree and in came one of those horrible plastic ones because we couldn't afford anything full, fancy, or realistic. We decorated that fake tree for years with a mishmash of ornaments: snowflakes the kids made in school out of Popsicle sticks and glitter, toys saved from McDonald's Happy Meals, a faded red-felt stocking I made in Sunday school at age nine, clothespin dolls, crocheted angels my aunt made for me and Mark as a wedding gift, and a soccer player, angel, and dancer made out of dough.

Right from the beginning, the ladies in our women's ministry wanted to start the tradition of an annual Christmas banquet. Year after year, women sat around beautifully decorated tables and told favorite Christmas traditions and stories. I sat with sweaty palms, listening to glorious tales of Swedish Christmases where women baked elaborate goodies dressed in hand-embroidered aprons and wore a crown of candles on their heads. Some hand-painted Christmas cards. Others had a theme tree in every room of their house—a teddy bear tree, an angel tree, an apple tree, a bow tree.

To me it seemed as if they were playing a game of "Can You Top This?" And I sat there knowing I had the tree no one would die for. My early impression was that everybody else seemed to have it all together and could do things perfectly. These women all seemed to represent the perfect wife, mother, and decorator. I worked hard to be a perfect pastor's wife, but as for artistic flair, I rivaled the person who can't chew gum and walk at the same time.

I tried to protect myself at these events by smiling and keeping my mouth full, making it impossible for me to share. None of my Christmas decorations matched, and the way I did things didn't match the style of the women in our congregation, many of whom I didn't know well. I decided I just needed to try harder. I was determined to have something that was a tradition in my family. For a couple of years I made a fish stew for Christmas Eve. Nobody would eat it. Then I tried chili and the kids hated it. I envied the families who sipped wonderful specialty drinks around the fireplace and sang carols after a delicious, traditional meal. We couldn't even find something we all liked to eat or drink. I desperately tried beef fondue—and they liked it! Finally, we had one family tradition in place.

One year the women's Christmas banquet was particularly spectacular. Children of the church sang a short program and then joined their mothers at the tables. My participating child was a growing preteen exhibiting the normal effects of raging hormones. I, as the parent of this dear child, could do nothing right, as was often and quickly pointed out. My obvious inadequacies and lack of general knowledge seldom went unnoticed or unmentioned.

Following in the routine of these affairs, people at each table told each other about their holiday traditions. Before long, a kind woman gently asked: "What are your Christmas traditions, dear?" The whole table leaned in to learn the sacred inner secrets of the pastor's family. My lovely child looked from face to face and with great poise said, "Nothing. We do absolutely nothing for Christmas."

Stunned silence and opened mouths circled the table. Every head turned in choreographed motion to see my face, which was now a rather vibrant shade of red.

Someone tried again. "Surely you have some little tradition?"

"Nope. We absolutely have none."

I was embarrassed beyond words. I didn't even try to salvage the moment or our reputations. They went on to the next person as I sat red-faced and fuming.

I found my voice on the way to the car—did I ever! I looked at my precious preteen and through clenched teeth reviewed our traditions. "Don't you remember those little German cookies that take hours and hours and hours for me to make, that are about a fourth of an inch big and break your teeth? Now that's a tradition! Don't you remember the Christmas Eves with that fish stew you all hated as a tradition? Don't you remember the sugar cookies we make every year? You all insist on mixing the different colors of frosting together and it turns out a yucky shade of gray. That's a Christmas tradition if I've ever heard of one!"

I wasn't finished. "What about the movie, *It's a Wonderful Life*? I make you watch it every year. When I make popcorn, you know what's coming. And it's a tradition for all of you to mock me when I cry and to say in a mimicky voice with the little girl, 'Look, Daddy, every time a bell rings, an angel gets its wings!' That's a tradition!"

After my spewed reminder, I said, "Now, what are our Christmas traditions?" And the reply was even more sarcastic: "That Dad's never home over Christmas." I was so angry, so shocked, I slammed the car door shut and drove home in silence.

It wasn't true, about Mark not being home, but that was my child's perception. There is no denying that December is a full month for a pastor. We're invited to so many events: private parties and staff parties, special programs and concerts and extra services. It seems like something is on the calendar every night. Mark does get home early on Christmas Eve, but not before he's participated in two of the four services held by our church.

It's always tricky finding the balance between a pastor taking care of the flock and a parent taking care of his children, and December is the most difficult month. After our ordeal at the banquet, Mark and I talked with our kids about the responsibilities and expectations of a pastor and about the effects of his work on his family. He pointed out that some parents have jobs that require a lot of travel and often miss soccer and little league games. But, in our family, their dad rarely misses any. He reminded them that being a pastor is a job with requirements, like any other job.

The church isn't that much different than our culture. Both pressure us to do more and get more and have more, with a sense of urgency to obtain perfection. An attitude of competitiveness and an inclination toward perfection in ministry, in parenthood, in womanhood, even in Christmas, often shows up in Christian articles and books. I found that if I am not deliberate in my thinking, my focus easily shifts from the birth of Christ to the busyness of holiday activities. I began to pray for wisdom concerning Christmas and began to focus on a way to simplify our celebration. I stopped comparing our family to others and our Charlie Brown tree to the perfectly decorated ones in the homes of our friends and church members. I gave up thinking I could please everyone who watched our lives. I let go of the insane idea of having a perfect anything, especially a perfect Christmas. Then, after a series of unexpected events, we had one: a perfectly wonderful Christmas.

It started in April with a very unusual dream. I'm not a person who sees visions or finds mysterious messages in my sleep, but I knew this one was different. I clearly saw a long, empty beach with pure-white sand. The beautiful blue-green ocean glittered with white-capped waves. The sound of water was like music. It was so colorful and so real I could smell the salt air and feel the sun's warmth. Then, I saw Jesus on this beach, happily swinging someone around in a circle, like Mark did with our kids when they were little, holding them in his arms as he twirled around and around. I knew it was Jesus when I looked at his laughing face and clear eyes, so filled with love. I couldn't exactly identify the person in his arms, but I woke knowing that it was either me or one of my daughters.

I stayed up the rest of the night, thinking about this incredibly peaceful dream. After seeing his face, I wondered how I could ever be afraid of anything, even death, if Jesus was like that. I was overwhelmed by the beauty and by the importance of what I had seen. Without knowing what, I knew that something very important was going to happen. I wasn't afraid; I was comforted. It was as if I was told, "All will be well; don't worry."

I pondered all this for a few days and finally told Mark about it. If something were to happen to me, I wanted him to know about the dream. The more I thought about it, I equated it to a near-death experience I've heard other people talk about, how they are no longer afraid of dying. For me, it was a comforting image for the question, "Where is God?"

The next month, on May 31, our 11-year-old daughter started vomiting. She'd had some fairly common stomach flu symptoms for a few days, but she woke up on Friday morning with dreadful pain. I got Rachel in to see the doctor for his first appointment and immediately he sent her to the hospital for an ultrasound. It seemed forever before a doctor told us she had acute appendicitis and that a rupture could occur at any time. That afternoon, as she was rolled into the operating room, the surgeon said, "It'll take about 45 minutes...I'm sure it's contained...we'll see you then."

Each minute seemed to slow down. Mark and I paced and prayed and hugged friends who came to the hospital to sit with us. Forty-five minutes passed; an hour, an hour and fifteen minutes, an hour and a half. I circled the waiting room remembering my dream. I wondered, "Is the Lord planning on taking Rachel home? Is that what he meant by my dream? Was he telling me she was going to die?"

The surgeon finally came out and told us her appendix had probably burst two days ago. They had done all they could do; now she was fighting for her life. Three different bacterias were raging in her little body. I spent every night at the hospital. By Tuesday I was exhausted and Rachel was in bad shape. That night, near midnight, I walked down the hall to the restroom. When I came back by the nurses' station, I was told the doctor had just called to let me know he and his wife were praying for our daughter. I was grateful, but I could feel the panic swelling within me. I was afraid I was going to lose my baby girl. And there was nothing I could do about it.

God answered our prayers and by Wednesday night, Rachel began to show improvement. By Thursday she was able to eat a little food, and a week later, fragile and gaunt, she left the hospital. Her eyes were sunken and discolored; she weighed only 60 pounds and resembled a child rescued from a concentration camp.

Slowly, Rachel gained strength and we decided to go ahead with our planned family vacation. Mark had to return to Fuller Seminary to speak for his doctoral program and we had scheduled a few extra days in California. I was walking exhaustion and Rachel was weak in a wheelchair. We all desperately needed a change.

On the second day of our vacation, Mark looked at me and said, "Take the day off. Be by yourself today and do whatever you'd like to do. I'll take the kids to Sea World." I quickly accepted his offer and knew exactly what I wanted to do. I went to the ocean.

I expected to lie on my towel and relax in the soothing breeze, lulled by the sound of the surf. Instead anger rushed through me. My emotions had been pinned down for so long that now, in this solitary place, they burst as violently and unexpectedly as my daughter's appendix. I felt that we had suffered enough traumas in life, to the point that I had only one requirement of God: "Just protect my husband and kids." I hadn't realized how terrified I had been during my daughter's illness. If she had shown any previous signs of pain or serious symptoms, I certainly would have taken her to the hospital immediately, before any rupture could have happened. Then after her surgery, no matter what they did, bacteria in the petri dishes kept growing. Unable to stop it, I watched the doctors' faith falter. Rachel survived by a slender thread, but I was not grateful. I was angry. Her near-death experience was just the latest in a series of losses.

My mother died just two years earlier without my getting to say goodbye. A vascular bundle in her brain had burst and by the time I got to her bedside, she was unconscious and on life support. It was quick and unexpected and I felt so helpless. Mark's beloved grandmother had died just the month before. Then, on the second anniversary of my mother's death, Mark's younger brother committed suicide. We had known for years that he suffered from deep depression and we had tried so hard to help him. Neither our efforts nor our prayers stopped him from taking his own life. And just recently, a church family close to us lost both a husband and son in a car accident. Death was all around us.

Now we had nearly lost our daughter. I really hadn't experienced a moment of time alone to feel how all this loss was affecting me. As my family played at Sea World, popping wheelchair wheelies and taking pictures of each other in front of fish tanks, I spent the day crying on my towel, reading my Bible, and lashing out at God for giving me a fresh vision that turned into a reality of yet another threat of death. I was not handling loss, or near loss, very well. I spent the rest of my time alone praying, seeking a sense of calm and reason.

The next day, we all decided to go the beach. Once again, I stretched out on my towel, exhausted and emotionally spent, unsure I could face the quiet again or the confusion of thoughts in my mind. Mark slept on a blanket next to me while our two oldest children searched for shells on the nearly deserted beach. I closed my eyes and felt the sun and moist salt air warm my bones. I listened to the song of gulls. A shadow fell across my face and I looked up to see our little eleven-year-old scarecrow standing nearby on pure-white sand. Blue-green waves crashed in perfect symmetry behind her solitary form. Blond curls danced and fluttered in the breeze. Thin and pale, my daughter was encircled by a halo of the sun's bright reflection. My eyes filled with tears and my throat grew taut in my effort to choke off sudden sobs. I knew what I was seeing.

My dream. God was showing me again that Rachel was not alone. Someone stood behind her, holding her. I couldn't see him now but I knew he was there. All the sense I sought the day before fell into place. Had my daughter lived or died, she was in the arms of Jesus. I thought if I loved her enough and tried hard enough, I could control, or at least protect, her destiny. Seeing her standing all alone on the beach, I knew as I had never known before that she did not belong to me. I wanted to own her, but she belonged to God. He loved her infinitely more than I ever had or could. In that moment, my anger was gone. I whispered, "I'm sorry for not trusting you," then leapt from my towel, ran to my baby, put my arms around her, and held her close.

A few months later, I learned that my daughter was not the only one in the arms of Jesus. Mark and I were alone in our van when we were hit by a car running a red light. Our vehicle slammed against the car next to us, flipped up and over, hit the pavement, and slid on the passenger side before landing upside down on the roof. Again, time seemed to slow down. Suspended in air, I thought, "I hope Mark is wearing his seat belt." Then, when the van collapsed and skidded along the pavement, I looked at the colors in the asphalt just inches from my face. I made myself close my eyes so I didn't have to watch my death. While neither of us escaped without months of pain and a series of surgeries, we escaped with our lives.

That following December we celebrated the best Christmas we'd ever had. It was the Christmas of second chances. How often do we get second chances in life? My daughter, Mark, and I had all been close to death and we were spared. We knew too well the deaths of family and friends, and from our experience it seemed that second chances were quite rare. We were alive, we were together. With a newly focused clarity, I didn't worry about ornaments that said, "Made in Taiwan" or mismatched decorations. I didn't send out Christmas cards. I didn't even think of making it "perfect."

A few days before Christmas, Mark and I hobbled through the mall to shop for gifts, just the two of us, walking slowly and gingerly. We linked our arms together, leaning on each other for support. We must have been a sorry sight, me in a neck brace and

Mark bent over and limping. It was a "Who's dragging who?" fore-shadow of growing old and gray together.

I thought of all the amazing things we shared in life. The times Mark and I prayed on our knees for one child or another, sick or scaring us with growing up. I thought of the times we prayed together about our lives in the ministry. Being linked arm in arm reminded me of the time I put my arm around him when his older brother died of leukemia; when he put his arm around me when I spread my mother's ashes in the mountains; when I put my arm around him as his younger brother was buried. How incredible it was to know the Lord had given us each other, to limp through life together, through the good and the bad. Linked arm in arm, we have gone through it.

On Christmas Day, I sat propped up in a chair next to the tree, the fake one I wouldn't want compared to a real Colorado pine. Mark said to the kids, "Tell us something you love about Christmas; tell us something about your ornaments on the tree." Every year I buy each child an ornament. They never match; they're a combination of glass and metal, porcelain and paper. The kids open them on Christmas day and hang them on our plastic tree.

Willingly, our children went around the whole tree talking about each of their ornaments and what they personally meant. They remembered the events of the year that matched the orna-ment. I listened and realized the uniqueness of our family. We did have traditions. Christmas *was* the gray frosting on the cookies; it *was* those little clothespin angels the kids made in first grade; it *was* the Popsicle-stick frames with school pictures glued in the middle; and it *was* the blue-glitter star made in fifth grade. This tree represented love to my children. It was a picture of their lives.

That was our favorite Christmas. We weren't wrapped up in getting things done on time or making things perfect. That day, I realized Christmas is about holding your children on your lap and telling them exactly what they mean to you. It's linking arms with your husband and spending an hour at the mall, reflecting on what it means to limp through life together, remembering all the special memories that belong just to the two of you. It's sitting at a meal together and drinking in the fact that Jesus was born in a manger, not in a mansion, for each and every one of us.

Christmas is remembering Jesus and what he did. Even as a senior pastor's wife, I never felt quite like I measured up. But I'm learning not to compare myself to others. I don't have to cook and decorate well to impress God. Christmas is not about me doing stuff but about what he did for me. He loves me just the way I am, flawed and imperfect. He loves me the way we love our Christmas tree. To us, it's beautiful. It's filled with perfect symbols of love and life. And no other can compare.

nine

Challenging, Changeless Grace

Chonda Pierce is a funny woman. Her laughter and her southern drawl can be heard above the noise of the crowd that usually surrounds her. Chonda's professional comedy career began with a five-year stint at Opryland USA as an impersonator of Miss Minnie Pearl. Witty monologues about her personal life quickly launched a successful solo career. Through her one-woman show and as a featured guest in the Women of Faith Conferences, Chonda has told her story to over one million people.

I had to wake up way before dawn one morning in order to meet Chonda's tour bus before it pulled out of Nashville. After a few hours of intermittent sleep, Chonda and I checked into a train-themed motel while her crew prepared for the evening concert in a local church. We sat cross-legged on a double bed and told stories of childhood and Christmas, giggling and crying over memories of the past.

Humor is the gift that enabled Chonda to survive, and then tell, a succession of family tragedies. Laughter may be the cornerstone of her performances, but faith in God is the cornerstone of her very existence.

CHONDA'S STORY

our red-felt stockings, trimmed in lace and white fur (even my brother's), with names stitched across the front—that's what I remember first when I think about my childhood Christmases. My grandmother had hand-sewn the stockings for my brother, two sisters, and me, and Momma hung them from the mantle in order from oldest to youngest: *Mike, Charlotta, Chonda, Cheralyn.* Daddy was a preacher and we were pretty poor, but those stockings symbolized a wealth of love and a lot of laughter. The trees we cut and decorated changed every year: tall trees, short trees, fat trees, and skinny trees. But those oversized red stockings remained the same and always hung in the same place.

The first thing we kids did on Christmas morning was race right to them. I don't know why it was so exciting; we always got the same thing—fruit, nuts, a handful of orange and black candies, and one really cool candy bar. Momma was as frugal as she was smart, and some of our Halloween candy was recycled in December by "Santa." Our stockings were always bulging with goodies—especially Mike's.

For several Christmases in a row, my brother found *four* candy bars in his stocking while we three sisters found none. Mike, with a lopsided grin on his face, shrugged and said, "I guess you girls just weren't that good this year." I finally figured out that he got up early, swiped *our* bars, and stuffed them into his own! Momma couldn't fuss at him, of course, because then we would know that Santa Claus wasn't real. She would wag her finger at Mike and say, "I'm sure Santa Claus intended for you to *share* those with your sisters." Now it seems so funny—just like a big brother to pull a stunt like that!

Usually, only one of us kids received a really great Christmas gift. Our family couldn't afford for everyone to do really well at the same time, but we didn't mind. When the baby of our family, Cheralyn, was ten, she got her heart's desire: a pink Barbie camper, pulled behind a pink Barbie car that was occupied by a couple of new Barbies. I had secretly and t-e-d-i-o-u-s-l-y labored for weeks on my present to her: hand-sewn outfits for the new dolls. On Christmas morning, all of us were so excited because we knew what was waiting for Cheralyn under the tree. The rest of us didn't do so hot, but we truly didn't care. Watching her sweet face dance with surprise and laughter as she tore into her pink treasure trove was our best gift.

One year, my older sister, Charlotta, hit the jackpot. I thought she was so sophisticated, wearing lipstick and eye shadow and constantly changing her hairstyle. She was the first to escape the "dress-alike" clothes Momma made for us girls. For months before December, all Charlotta talked about was Clairol Hot Rollers. When she opened them up on Christmas Day, we all shrieked with joy. Goodness only knows why. The things looked like cylinders of torture designed by space aliens, all prickly and pokey, lined up in their little plastic case.

When my turn came for a good gift year, I got an Easy-Bake oven. I suspect Momma was hoping I would become domestic. (Nice try, but it didn't work.) The oven came with little cake mixes, but I added all kinds of other stuff to them and used it like a chemistry set. Eventually I blew the whole thing up. Years later, I got a real chemistry set, but it wasn't nearly as much fun.

Regardless of who got the best present, we could always count on the candy in the stockings. We'd count the number of pieces and sort them by color, and then race back to check the toes to make sure we hadn't missed any. We'd spend the rest of the day laughing and teasing each other, eating, and singing carols. I loved Christmas with my brother and sisters and couldn't imagine it being any other way. But one day, suddenly, it all changed.

On a hot July morning, in stifling humidity and drizzling rain, my sister Charlotta, now a twenty-year-old young woman, drove from our home in Ashland City to her job in Nashville. On an overpass her car hydroplaned on wet asphalt and crashed into an oncoming vehicle. Charlotta was instantly killed. Our family could hardly breathe during her funeral, both from the oppressive heat and the unspeakable sorrow crushing our hearts.

Five months later, when Momma and I opened up the box of Christmas ornaments, the first thing we saw was Charlotta's stocking. We both gasped. I sat down, stunned. *What are we supposed to do with this?* I wondered. Without a word, Momma set the stocking aside and we finished decorating. Then, Momma hung the three stockings of her living children in a line on the mantle: *Mike, Chonda, Cheralyn.*

Momma hoped the absence of Charlotta's stocking would help us avoid memories of her death. But later that evening, Cheralyn and I agreed that Charlotta was still very much a part of our family. We wanted the symbol of her life with us, so we got her stocking and hung it between *Mike* and *Chonda*. Some days, we faced her stocking just fine. Other days, someone couldn't handle it and took it down for a little while. So whether they were visible or out of sight, our treasured stockings, once designs of love and life, now reminded us of grief, separation, and death.

Without any planning on that first Christmas Day without her, each of us wrote notes to Charlotta and dropped them into her empty red sock. We wrote of our love, of how we missed her. We promised never to forget her. No one told us to do this; it just happened. It helped us survive the devastating blow of her death.

By the next Christmas, another stocking was missing from the lineup, but for a happy reason. My brother got married. Mike and his bride, Dorris, hung their childhood stockings side by side in their little apartment. That left two stockings at home—one for me and one for Cheralyn.

But that wasn't the only change that year; something else was missing from our home: my father. He disappeared for most of November, then dropped by on Christmas Day "to say hello," and to bring a little gift to Cheralyn and me. For the life of me, I don't remember what he brought, but I still remember how odd it seemed to see him awkwardly standing in our house. I remember the weird tension between us. I felt like saying, "You are interfering with us trying to survive over here. If you're going to go, just go."

I was seventeen, boisterous and loud-mouthed, seething with anger over our father abandoning us, grieving over the loss of my sister, missing my married brother, and wanting to protect my baby sister. At fourteen, Cheralyn was everything I seemed not to be: lovely, quiet, and humble in spirit. She was so tenderhearted and quick to cry, every Lassie episode and every tacky TV romance movie dissolved her in a puddle of tears. Our whole family teased her mercilessly, but mostly we cherished her. Cheralyn was extremely saddened by our father's departure, and she was equally glad to see him whenever he showed up. Not me.

My life seemed staked to the middle of a whirlwind. My father's appearances just added to the fury of my internal storm. Rumors and suspicion about him swirled around me. Bitterness and resentment spun circles in my head, and grief and loneliness roared in my ears. I had known for years that my parents' marriage was troubled, and I heard accusations of my father's infidelity. I wasn't hoping for a happy family reunion, but if it had been my year for the "really good" Christmas, I would have asked for the gift of truth. I wanted the truth about my father's life. I wanted to hear

him say, "This is why I'm leaving; this is why it's best for me to go."
I wanted a real, adult conversation with him. I never got it. It never
happened.

Since Mike and Dad were both gone, Momma, Cheralyn, and
I tried really hard to make that Christmas as merry as possible. We
strung popcorn, glued paper ornaments, played carols all day,
every day, for weeks. In spite of my own emotional roller coaster,
I tried to help Momma. We no longer received a housing
allowance from the church, we no longer resided in the parsonage,
we were no longer the "Pastor's Family." Momma scrambled to
get a job, eventually working the night shift in a nursing home,
and I found part-time work after school. We needed money for
things like food, gasoline, and house payments, but Momma and
I also wanted to make Christmas great for Cheralyn. We wanted
to turn that cold, dark December into something special for our
baby girl. We never had a clue it would be her last. Four months
later, in the warmth of April, she was diagnosed with leukemia.
Twenty-one days later, in the sunshine of May, she died.

Twenty-two months separated the deaths of my two sisters,
hardly enough time for the grass to grow on the first grave. Hardly
enough time to let go of Charlotta before we were at the cemetery
again, saying goodbye to Cheralyn. I watched green-shirted
strangers shovel dirt onto her lowered casket, then looked at
Momma and very deliberately said, "Good grief. We're dropping
like flies." We both laughed, but it hurt—like trying to breathe
with broken ribs. Momma put her arms around me and forced me
close to her chest. She knew just where that laughter had come
from and that a much-needed cry would follow. I loved both my
sisters more than life itself, and I couldn't imagine my life without
either of them in it. I could not imagine ever laughing again—
really laughing, the way I always laughed with them.

My life slipped into what I call a "blessed fog." A thick covering of numbness, quiet and impenetrable, surrounded me. I
floated through the minutes and hours of each day before, during,
and following Cheralyn's funeral, unfeeling and detached in a

cloud of isolation. In the humid summer heat, Momma and I had a big yard sale, then moved what little was left of our belongings into a one-bedroom apartment. I started back to school, but felt no motivation. Life was hell on earth, the pits. I was penniless and miserable. Sometimes Momma would ask, "What are you going to do? You could get a little part-time job, you know." But I didn't. I freeloaded off her as much as an 18-year-old college student can freeload off a mother who had next to nothing.

The days and weeks slowly ticked by, and, inevitably, December came again. When the two of us drug out the box of Christmas decorations, we found the stockings, right on top: a little ornamental one with Mike's name on it (just big enough for a candy bar), and the three large, red-felt stockings stitched with the names *Charlotta, Cheralyn,* and *Chonda.* I felt sick to my stomach and turned my head away. I got busy with our "tree." Two large, tropical plants left over from Charlotta's and Cheralyn's funerals had flourished and grown jungle-like in the empty space of our living room. Momma and I couldn't afford to buy a Christmas tree of any size or shape, so I shoved them together and christened them "Blue Spruce" before hanging ornaments between the leaves.

I stood back to check out my obvious lack of Martha Stewart decorating skills. I sighed and said to myself as much as to Momma, "This is pitiful." I expected to hear a chuckle from Momma and glanced in her direction. She was looking at her four childrens' stockings laid out on the floor. The words flew out of my mouth. "This is the most pathetic thing I have ever seen." I picked them all up, intending to put them back in the box, but Momma gently took the *Chonda* stocking out of my hand and draped it on the tree. Only mine. I looked at it and said, "Well, *that's* the saddest thing I've ever seen in my whole life."

Momma studied it a moment. "Oh, no," she whispered. "That's the most *beautiful* thing I have ever seen." I could only see three missing stockings. Momma saw one beautiful stocking—*alive*! I was still alive and she was still a mother. Her love for me in those few words was one of the best Christmas presents of my life. At that moment, the cloud of numbness that had protected me since Cheralyn's death disappeared. I stood in the light of my mother's love, able to breathe and feel again.

On that first Christmas morning for two, with one lone stocking draped on a tropical Blue Spruce, I handed my mother a tiny box. She untied the green bow, lifted the lid, and removed a folded piece of paper that she smoothed out with her hands. She admired the borders I had decorated and colored with crayons and markers. Then her eyes focused in the center of the page. I had printed in big, block letters: *I GOT A JOB.*

Nothing could have been better. She read it and cried. Then she laughed. She laughed at my hand-crafted announcement and laughed with relief. We were so broke. And she was so worried about me. One small box with one small piece of paper and four big words, I GOT A JOB, was the only present my Momma received that year. But I guess it meant a lot to her because every Christmas she still hangs that little box on her tree.

I knew how badly Momma needed the help, so the week before Christmas I had found a job as a desk clerk at a motel. Naturally, as the newest employee, I was given the crummiest hours. I had to work on Christmas Eve and on Christmas Day, but so did my mother. On Christmas morning, after she opened her little box, we ate breakfast together, then I went off to work and she went off to bed to rest up for her next shift.

I was actually glad to spend the day working at the motel. The holidays are tough on people who are grieving and most people didn't know what to do with us. Friends invited us into their homes to share big Christmas dinners with their families, but it was miserable, sitting there with their aunts, uncles, cousins, brothers, and sisters. It was too painful a reminder of our own past Christmases. The chatter and clatter of everybody around me—the stuff I used to think of as celebration—became noise. I wanted silence in my life. It was better to go to work.

Tallying receipts in a motel on Christmas Day was something I never expected. Until I was seventeen, my family always attended a Christmas morning church service, went home, opened presents, ate a wonderful meal together, and lived out one of Norman Rockwell's paintings. In three short years, all that changed. Now I sat at a front desk and watched other families come and go and wondered, *Why aren't they around some tree and why isn't a turkey cooking in their kitchen oven?* I saw truckers park their rigs and stride in for a plate of turkey and dressing. It was the right stuff to eat but everything about it seemed wrong. I watched the waitress hustle through the restaurant, serving an endless rotation of customers. I admired the friendly way she greeted her guests, took their orders, and then efficiently and quickly delivered their meals. But I was most impressed by the fact that she had volunteered to work that day so other waitresses with families could stay at home on Christmas. She gave a gift of kindness to both strangers and coworkers. And in a roundabout way, she gave me a gift. She showed me that Christmas can be spent in many ways. Not all gifts cost money and not all are wrapped in paper. And I wasn't the only one grieving on Christmas Day. Momma and I had that in common, and we had each other. Even struggling to survive, we still had the gift of life. And turkey in a truckstop wasn't *so* bad.

After a long day, I got home just in time to give Momma a hug as she left for her night shift at the nursing home. In the silence of our little apartment, I sat and thought about my Christmas. No brother, no sisters, no father, no laughter around a big table. No tree (well, a tropical bush). One stocking, instead of four. The isolated shape of that pathetic red sock broke my heart.

Through my tears, I looked over at our nativity set. Its beauty and simplicity captured me. The painted faces and glazed eyes of Mary and Joseph made me wonder how happy they would have been if they had known how drastically their lives would change in the next thirty-three years.

Then the realization flooded over me: God knew. When Mary said yes, God knew what she would have to endure; knew she would feel the barbs of gossip and tremble in fear of the future. God knew she wouldn't fully understand the reasons and reality of her life; knew her heart would break at the foot of her Son's cross. Knowing all of what was ahead for Mary, God still called her "blessed among women."

God knew I would be alone on this Christmas Day, looking at a porcelain nativity and one lone stocking. God knew my life would be changed by the oting of goooip, uncertainty of my future, sorrow for an absent father, grief over lost sisters. And still I would be blessed among women. Because, like Mary, I believed in the promise delivered in the stable. I trusted in the Savior laid in a manger. God knew I would find peace in the presence of a Child called the Comforter. And that will never change.

ten

When Christmas Is a Dreaded Day

Ann Weems is widely admired as a poet who draws from the heritage of Scripture to give voice to the soul. She is highly regarded as a speaker, liturgist, worship designer, and seminar leader for denominational, ecumenical, and interfaith conferences, seminars, and celebrations. In 1996, she was the recipient of the Distinguished Writer Award from the Presbyterian Writers Guild.

An acclaimed author, Ann has written Advent and Lenten poetry, litanies, and plays for worship. *Psalms of Lament* is a collection of psalm-inspired poetry over the death of her son, and her latest book, *Putting the Amazing Back in Grace,* is an impassioned call for a renewed faith and a sense of justice in the church.

Frequently on the road as a keynote speaker, guest poet, and workshop leader, Ann returns to her home in St. Louis and her husband, Don, a retired Presbyterian clergyman.

ANN'S STORY

*S*now fell before morning and continued to fall as St. Louis awoke, white-blanketed and exquisitely silent. Since Todd's death I appreciate silence more than ever. Something is sacred in the quiet, something I long for, something I need, especially in the blaring noise of Christmas.

Oh, God, how can I go out into this world and face the holiday racket? How can I go out shopping for presents after what has happened? How can I bake cookies and write cards and wish everyone "Merry Christmas!" as though my son had not been killed that August night? How can Christmas ever be merry again? How can I go through the motions or pretend everything is just fine when it will never again be fine?

It's Advent and at this time last year I was filled with exuberance. I busied myself with wrapping presents and decorating the tree and making cheese straws for the Christmas open house. I played a CD of Christmas carols and looked forward to commemorating each and every Advent day. But this year...how can I celebrate Christmas this year without Todd? *Oh, Todd, how can our lives go on without you?*

As if to answer my pain, snow fell faster and faster; bigger and bigger flakes raced to cover everything in sight, snow on snow on snow. In spite of myself, in spite of clouds bulging with more snow, in spite of my heart frozen in pain, these words came into my mind: *This is the day the Lord has made. Let us rejoice and be glad in it.* Rejoice and be glad in the silence of this exquisitely beautiful day, this exquisitely beautiful, stunning, God-made rejoicing day!

This was the same unbidden bit of Scripture that came to me as I awoke the morning after a gang of youths killed Todd. On that morning, the sun was bright, and I still dull with sleep thought: *This is the day the Lord has made. Let us rejoice and be glad in it.* Then I remembered: *Todd is dead, beaten to death on his twenty-first birthday.* The verse seemed nearly cruel. How could I rejoice that day?

Now, four months later, I struggled to rejoice in a beautiful, snowy Advent morning. *No! No, I will not rejoice and be glad! I will mourn and be sad. Let the rest of them rejoice! My son is dead, and it's not fair, and it's not right and I have no rejoicing in me...no rejoicing in me...*

Stirring sounds of morning began: my beloved husband, Don, shaving, eleven-year-old Heather calling down to ask if school had been canceled because of snow. I flipped on the TV and heard the hyper weather channel people announcing no cancellation of schools, just soft snow and plowed main arteries. I decided to drop Heather off at school and then go to the grocery store before the storm got any worse.

We stepped out into a winter wonderland and once more I thought: *An exquisitely beautiful God-made day!* A neighbor emerged from his house and waved to us. "Isn't this great?!" he called. We waved back and shouted: "Great!"

Heather laughed and said, "I love it!" I smiled at her. She looks more like her brother Todd than her brothers David or Stuart. She shares his dark, dark hair and deep brown smiling eyes. I thought, *She's much too young to know such pain.*

"The cemetery will be covered in snow," she said quietly and unexpectedly, as if she read my mind or shared my thoughts.

"Yes," I answered. "I bet it's gorgeous out there." I had been surprised that the cemetery was so lovely. After Todd's funeral I never wanted to even think about the cemetery, much less actually go there. But, gradually, I found myself drawn to it, found myself seeking its peacefulness, driving there to be near to Todd even though in my heart and soul I knew Todd was not there. I used to repeat to myself, *He is not here. He is with God,* but this is the place we left his young body on the August morning of his funeral, and this is the place we sought peace.

At school, Heather jumped out of the car, then leaned back in through the window to say, "Don't cry, Mom. I love you."

I smiled at her. "I love you, too," I said, "all to pieces!"

My precious girl. I've got to do something to make this a good Christmas for her. And for David, David who had to identify Todd's body, David who had to phone us in Maine, David who met us at the airport, David who, almost immediately after the funeral, went off alone to college in Oberlin, Ohio. And for Stuart, Stuart who was working in Minneapolis, Stuart who had to spend two days there alone with his pain before he could get transportation home. *Oh, God, save my children,* I cried.

And Don, Don, a pastor who got up every morning and went to the church to minister. I'll never know how he got through those first months. How must he feel now during these days of Advent? He hasn't had the luxury of hiding from public scrutiny. After Todd's death, I canceled all my speaking engagements. I had nothing to say. What will Don say when he steps to the pulpit each Advent Sunday? *Oh God, be with him…and be with the children, and oh, God, be with me!*

The grocery store parking lot was jammed with cars and people stocking up in case the snowstorm worsened. Stacks of bagged salt to melt road ice blocked the walkway outside the door. People ran through the snow from their cars laughing as I had done not too long ago. Spurts of laughter were so natural to our family but now our laughter was gone. I envied the lightheartedness around me.

Inside the store, and even before the automatic door slid completely shut, I heard Christmas music. Bing Crosby was dreaming of a white Christmas, just like the ones he used to know. *I might have a white Christmas, but it won't be like the ones I used to know. Todd won't be here. Todd will never be here again.* Uninvited tears burned my eyes. *Oh dear God, not again; don't let me fall apart in the grocery store. Don't let me see anyone I know! Just let me get my groceries and get out of here!*

I wheeled my cart up and down aisle after aisle, looking for items that made any kind of sense. *Who cares, who cares, who cares? Who cares about eating?* "Eat," our family doctor said. "You've got to be there for your family." He was right, and I promised. All of us loved Todd, all of us suffered the loss, but I had no appetite. Mostly, I wanted to sit in a rocking chair and rock my life away.

Soup, soup would be good for a snowy day, I thought. *Get soup, enough for several days. French bread goes well with soup. What else? Concentrate. You can do this. Tacos. Heather likes tacos. Maybe hamburgers and frozen French fries, anything easy. Hot chocolate! Marshmallows...the little ones. Comfort food. Get it in the cart and get out of here!*

The first time I went to the grocery store after Todd was killed, I was completely unprepared for the misery of it. It was such an ordinary thing to do. It was the kind of thing done by mothers of sons who were not killed. How could Todd be dead, and how could I be going to the grocery store a week later? How could all these people be walking around doing ordinary things when Todd was dead? I didn't want to be at the grocery store; I wanted to be at the Wailing Wall!

I prayed most ardently at the grocery store. *Let me, O God, put these groceries in my cart as quickly as possible and make my way out. Keep me, O God, from running into someone kind and sympathetic with tears in their eyes. Before that happens, get me out of here, O God.*

I was putting the hot chocolate box into the basket when it happened. I had shopped my way through "White Christmas" and "Jingle Bells." And "Chestnuts Roasting on an Open Fire" followed by Nat King Cole's "Santa Claus Is Coming to Town" and Elvis' "Blue Christmas." Then, suddenly, I heard:

> *What Child is this, who, laid to rest, on Mary's lap is*
> *sleeping?*
> *Whom angels greet with anthems sweet, while shep-*
> *herds watch are keeping?*
> *This, this is Christ, the King, whom shepherds guard*
> *and angels sing.*
> *Haste, haste to bring Him laud, the Babe, the Son of*
> *Mary.*

I bolted to the nearest and shortest checkout stand, nodded as the clerk attempted pleasant conversation, paid, and left. I put the groceries in the trunk, returned the cart, and got in my car. I couldn't shut the door quickly enough. I hurriedly put on my seatbelt, found the tape I knew was somewhere close at hand, shoved it into the player, and started the engine. Tears were flowing now. I grabbed at tissues and repeatedly wiped my eyes so I could see to drive. I knew what to expect and I was ready to hear it. Todd. Todd, whistling, "What Child Is This?"

How many times in his life had I heard him whistling? His pure whistling that always made me smile. Todd, coming home from school, Todd coming home from work, Todd coming home...up the walk, the sound of the key, the sound of his voice, "Mom?" Todd...coming home.

Last summer, Todd compiled this tape as something to hear while he did some painting at the church. He included "What Child Is This?" only it wasn't a professional recording, it was Todd himself whistling the tune. I kept it in my car, playing it over and over until I couldn't stand the pain of it anymore. It was so full of life, and he was lifeless now, and I felt lifeless, too, so I had put it away for a very long time.

The previous Christmas Todd had asked me what my favorite Christmas carol was. I told him, "What Child Is This?" He said it was his favorite, too. "How funny is that!" he laughed.

When I heard the song in the grocery store, in my head I heard Todd whistling. As I drove out of the parking lot, the words haunted me. "What Child Is This? What child is this? What child is this!" His whistling was so alive. *Why, O God, did this happen?* I was blinded by tears and didn't want to go home in such a mess. I wanted to drive for a while. Don and Heather would be horrified if they knew I was out on this stormy day but the roads were clear and the snow had practically stopped. On the spur of the moment I headed for Our Lady of the Snows, a Catholic shrine that displays lighted scenes from the Christmas story. Each Advent season hundreds of thousands of lights illuminate the nativity sculptures. Every night hundreds of cars creep through the two-mile length of the Way of the Lights.

All the way to Our Lady of the Snows, I played Todd's whistling. It was as if he was in the car with me. Then, I asked God why Todd couldn't be in the car with me. *Why can't he be here now and why can't we be sharing this, and why can't he be whistling in this snowy silence as we drive?*

It was peaceful at the shrine, quiet and serene. Only five or six other cars were there, supposing like me that this wintry morning was a good time to see the figures without the rush of traffic. I drove slowly and looked intently. When I got to Mary and the Child, I stopped. I looked at Mary's face, but she was looking at the Child as if she was saying, "What Child is this?" I reached the exit then circled back and re-entered again. This time, when I stopped in front of Mary and the Child, I asked her, "Did you know my son was killed, too? Did you know?" I asked. "Did you?"

Snow began falling again and I turned toward home. Todd whistled until I could no longer bear hearing his voice. I ejected the tape just as a radio voice sang, "I'll be home for Christmas." *But you won't!* I sobbed. *You won't be home for Christmas! You'll never be home for Christmas again. You'll never carry in the tree and you'll never again help decorate it; you'll never usher at the Christmas Eve service, you'll never sit on the steps and wait until Dad calls you and Stuart and David and Heather to come in and open your stockings. You'll never see the manger on the mantel and you'll never open the shoes your father bought for you when we were in Maine, the shoes that still sit on his closet shelf, and you'll never again taste the eggnog and the turkey and the chess pie. You'll never kiss me and smile at me with those dark brown eyes after you've opened my presents to you, and I'll never hug your lean six-four frame again!*

The tears...again. Tissues...again. Sorrow...again. The snow fell in fat flakes on my windshield, and I wondered if I should have ventured so far out. I thought of Our Lady of the Snows and I was glad I had come. I thought of Mary and realized what joy she must have felt as she showed the Child to the shepherds. I remembered my joy at the birth of each of our children. Christmas was about birth, I thought, not death.

Calmly, again, I pushed the tape back into the player. Todd's voice whistled, "What Child Is This?" and I answered him out loud in the car. "This, this is Christ the King, whom shepherds guard and angels sing. Haste, haste to bring him laud, the Babe, the son of Mary."

What Child is this? I knew! He is Emmanuel. God with us!

He was born so we would know the good news that God is with us. In all our years of family celebrations, we celebrated just that at Christmas time: God is with us. Our celebration never centered on people but on God coming into our world. I couldn't think of a year when we needed to feel the presence of God more than in this year. We were never needier. This year more than ever before we understood the words from Isaiah: *The people who walked in darkness have seen a great light.* This year we walked in the darkness of our grief, but in the midst of our sorrow over Todd's death came good news: The Holy Child is born! Emmanuel! Advent! God COMES and is with us! We have seen a great light, the light of hope and promise.

By the time Stuart and David arrived home, our city was deep in fresh, white snow. When we went to the cemetery to visit Todd's grave, we drove though a frozen world, the only car venturing out. The steep, icy road made getting close to the grave impossible. We parked, intending to walk the rest of the way, but as we stepped out of the car we found ourselves sliding backwards on the sloping hill. David was determined to make it, so the rest of us loaded his arms with poinsettias and a wreath and stood by the car watching. He skated up the slope, nearly fell, slid down, struggled forward, and slid again. While we gasped and cheered, he gained a few inches of ground, slid back, and with undiminished determination, started again. He had not gained very much ground when he laughed and said, "I bet Todd's getting a kick out of this!"

We all began to laugh. David kept going, falling, laughing, sliding, but miraculously holding on to the flowers and wreath until he finally made it. His return to the car required nothing more than one single slide down the hill. We all got in the car laughing and Don called out, "Merry Christmas, Todd."

Of course, there were more tears, but there was also an abundance of laughter as we celebrated together the birth of this Child who came to bring light into our darkness. We knew how very much the Christ Child was sent *for* us. "What Child is this?" He is the Light of the world, the Babe, the son of Mary.

NOT CELEBRATE?

Not celebrate?
Your burden is too great to bear?
Your loneliness is intensified during this
   Christmas season?
Your tears seem to have no end?
Not celebrate?
You should lead the celebration!
You should run through the streets
   to ring the bells and sing the loudest!
You should fling the tinsel on the tree,
   and open your house to your neighbors,
      and call them in to dance!
For it is you above all others
   who know the joy of Advent.
It is unto you that a Savior is born this day,
   One who comes to lift your burden from your
shoulders,
   One who comes to wipe the tears from your eyes.
You are not alone,
   for he is born this day to you.

   —Ann Weems

eleven

A New Tradition

Connie grew up in Ohio, the third of eight children born to her homemaker mom and her mail carrier dad. When she married just after college, she dreamed of replicating the happiness she saw between her parents. But poor choices and uncontrollable circumstances led from one disaster to another and the dream was destroyed.

Even the strongest woman can be brought to her knees by tragedy and loss. Even the strongest can be weak with failure. At those times, the strength of the Lord can lift a woman out of the ashes, renewed and purified by the "refiner's fire." Connie is one such woman.

She told her story from a small town in Indiana, and began with the Christmas that went up in smoke—literally.

CONNIE'S STORY

"Merry Christmas," I thought as my husband and I sat in my brother-in-law's van and watched flames devour our 100-year-old farmhouse. Our twin daughters slept in our laps while the fire's wind whipped burning Holly Hobbie curtains through shards of window glass. A little more than an hour before, I had smelled smoke, and now everything, everything, was gone.

It was Christmas Eve. Jennifer and Jill had recently celebrated their first birthdays and we realized they would not remember this home, this night. No pictures would exist to show them where they lived, what they looked like in their first year of life, or how funny their mommy and daddy looked at their wedding. Nothing was saved but our lives: our home, our cat, our possessions— burned. I silently asked God, "Why?" and almost immediately felt a check in my spirit as the Lord brought to mind, "All things work together for good to them that love God, to them who are the called according to his purpose" (Romans 8:28 KJV). I struggled to trust that promise.

As we drove away from the ashes of our belongings, I stared back at the people lining the road, spectators to our tragedy. I resented such public curiosity about something so private. Thank God, I had no inkling how much more of my private life would be subject to public scrutiny.

After the fire, everything changed. Some changes were expected, like building and furnishing a new house. Other changes proved as devastating as the fire. The good thing was that our babies, seemingly unfazed by the upheaval, blossomed like the lovely spring flowers I planted beside the garage of our new house. I watched our daughters' growth with mixed feelings.

Being a stay-at-home mom was my ideal, especially after the twins were born, but my husband had a very different opinion. When I expressed my desire to give up teaching, he snapped, "Well, I don't like to go to work, either. We need the money; you're not quitting."

Continuing to work wasn't that easy. In order to qualify for a permanent teaching license, I had to complete my Master's Degree within the next few years. So, I continued to drive 45 minutes each way to school, pursued my degree through night classes, and took care of our home and two young children pretty much on my own. Like so many women who sense trouble in a marriage, I ignored the evidence of my husband's discontent and apathy and made excuses for his aloofness. He rarely spent time at home and when he did, he kept busy with his own interests rather than helping with chores or spending time with his family.

Three years passed. I finished my last master's class, our home was comfortable, and I delighted in each phase of my daughters' lives. My personal stress was considerably less, and I tenaciously held to the hope that if my husband would only grow up and take more responsibility, the stress on our marriage could be reduced as well.

Then fall came and the girls turned four. I was still recovering from my dearly loved grandfather's recent death when winter ushered in the final stage of my father's fight against cancer. In December, we celebrated the birth of Christ, unaware that it was the last Christmas my husband would live at home. In the spring, he left us.

When our farmhouse was destroyed, I thought feeling any deeper sense of devastation would be impossible. Now I knew better. I was losing the core of my life; and, again, people watched and speculated on my private tragedy. Again, I asked God, "Why?" and wondered how divorce could fit into his promise to make all things work together for good. As before, I had to trust that God could be my strength.

The next few months were an emotional bonfire. My hope for reconciliation was consumed by revelations of my husband's blatant lies and habitual duplicity. His burning contempt gutted all that made me identifiable to myself: marriage, personal and economic security, relationships to extended family and mutual friends, and, especially, every shred of self-esteem. I was stunned that someone I trusted so implicitly could so insensitively abuse that trust. "What if's" plagued my mind. What if the girls chose to live with their father and his girlfriend? What if this divorce leads them to delinquency or pits them against one parent or the other? When this is behind me, what if no one ever wants to date me? What if I live alone for the rest of my life?

Our divorce was finalized just before Christmas, just in time for me to register the brutal realities of "reasonable visitation" shared with someone who wasn't reasonable. My daughters were scheduled to be with their father on Christmas Eve and my heart froze at the thought of being separated from them. We had shared all of life's important events together and this was the first of many occasions to come that I would be excluded.

Christmas Eve afternoon, I cheerfully waved as the girls left with their dad to go to their grandma's, but my cheeriness was phony. In truth, bitterness devoured me. My ex-husband's girlfriend had been a part of his life much longer than I wished to know, and now she was spending this special evening with my daughters, in a home I once considered my own, with people who had been my family for ten years. I went back inside my house, closed the door, and heard nothing but emptiness. I tried to see the day from the girls' point of view. They were old enough now to talk about everything—what they wanted Santa to bring, wrapping paper we bought at the store, the deer we saw standing by the side of the road. As they dressed to go, they bubbled over with the excitement of being at Grandma's for a big night, while I struggled with my hatred for the "other woman" and with the pain of being discarded.

Memories of past traditions bombarded me as I walked through the silent house. I tried not to think of being alone. I wrapped the last of the gifts and picked up remnants of five-year-old playthings. I baked their favorite cookies and made food to take to my sister's the next day. I anticipated the girls' return and our Christmas morning together, spent the rest of the evening watching television and puttering around the house and, despite my bravest effort, crying. To escape thoughts of my own circumstances, I concentrated on Jesus and how the first Christmas actually was a sacrifice as well as a gift. I tried to imagine his heavenly home and all he must have given up. He left glory—and I don't think I really understand what all that means—but for him to become human meant he understood sacrifice. I tried to think of all that but got stuck on my own losses. I tried to honestly confront the feelings that followed the destruction of my marriage. I hated what was happening to me. I didn't deserve this. I had been faithful, a good wife. Why was I the one alone on this night?

Around midnight, their daddy brought the sleeping girls home and carried them to their beds. He refused to acknowledge me or answer any of my questions about their evening, as if I didn't exist. Jill was clutching a pair of leather Isotoners with a gift tag bearing my name. My former mother-in-law sent them to me for Christmas and I remember them well. Those gloves were the last gift I ever received from my husband's family, the last acknowledgement of my marriage.

After the girls were in bed, their father brusquely carted armloads of presents from his car to my living room. Then, without a moment of kindness left behind, he was gone. That dark

Christmas Eve, I put away any lingering ideas of ever hearing gratitude for our ten years of life together or for my being his children's mother.

My ex-husband did accept my invitation to come back on Christmas morning to be with the girls when they opened their gifts. My intention was that his presence would make as nearly a normal family Christmas as possible. But from the moment of his arrival, he spent more time looking at his watch than at his daughters. He was a spectator of their lives, not a participant; he wasn't willing to be involved, he was obligated to be present. His behavior that morning was a glimpse of things to come. Over the years, he missed seeing the miracle of their lives, whether swimming, cheerleading, playing softball, singing in recitals, crying when boys broke their hearts, or achieving minor and major victories. He missed all those irretrievable moments.

I will never forget that first Christmas morning after the divorce. After their father left, I coaxed the girls and their new cache of Barbie dolls to the breakfast table and listened to them chatter about their night at Grandma's. Every few minutes they glanced my way to see how I was reacting. I really wanted to say how hurtful my exclusion felt, but I knew right then that they needed the freedom to say whatever was on their minds. I knew I could not use them as a sounding board for my anger or grief toward their father or his family. I knew that as they got older, they would be more aware of the difficulty caused by their allegiance to two households. I didn't want any facet of my daughters' lives to be off limits because of me. They needed to feel secure more than I needed to voice my opinion.

I tried hard after that to keep a civil relationship with their father and members of his family, even though I found myself on the receiving end of constant verbal attacks. I admit to lashing back in anger and frustration. Sometimes, my desperate need for retribution and validation overtook any desire to control my tongue. I tried, really tried, to protect the girls from volatile conversations. I wanted to rise above the reality but our reality was often grim.

At first, I couldn't count on child support. My ex-husband conveniently refused to acknowledge that his erratic checks barely covered the cost of child care. Yet, if I purchased anything new for my house and he saw it, I could expect snide remarks that his money must have purchased it. Eventually the courts forced him to pay on a regular basis, and I stopped worrying if we'd make it every month. After that, there was no asking him to chip in for extra things for the girls, like church camp or sports equipment. He'd shrug and say, "Not my responsibility" with that hands-up-in-the-air gesture, like "too bad."

The girls and I grew never to expect my ex-husband's physical or financial help, but his indifference created unfair and lopsided circumstances. The responsibility to take them to their appointments and school activities always fell to me. I never had any time to myself until they were in bed for the night. To say I was tired, physically and emotionally, is an understatement! I remember him calling late one night to talk with the girls, but they were already in bed. Before he hung up, I asked if he would take Jill to a doctor's appointment since I had an important meeting at school. Once again, he started in on his list of lame excuses. Sick of his attitude, I lambasted him, unaware that Jill was in the next room, listening.

Frustrated, I slammed the phone down. Before the sound died away, Jill walked around the corner. Her bottom lip quivered as she whispered, "It makes me feel real bad that nobody wants to take me to the doctor." My heart broke. I knew then that Jill and Jennifer were the ones being unfairly affected. Holding her in my arms, I apologized. "I'm sorry, Jilly. I'll always take you wherever you need to go." Never again did I ask her father for help.

Their father's near total detachment from his own daughters on a day-to-day basis dumbfounded me, and I really couldn't understand his impossible Christmas demands. He wanted the girls on Christmas Eve for his family's big party, plus he wanted them to spend the night so they could open their gifts with him on Christmas morning. The fact that they were supposed to be with me on Christmas morning was irrelevant to him. Compromise or a logical discussion was not in his makeup, so we had to go to court to settle the holiday custody issue. I meant to protect the twins from our bitterness toward each other, but obviously I didn't do a very good job.

A few weeks before Christmas, I overheard Jennifer talking on the phone with a friend. "Yeah," she said, "me, too. I can't wait for Christmas. I go to my dad's every Christmas Eve and then we open presents here with my mom on Christmas morning." She paused for a moment, "The only thing...well, truthfully...I hate Christmas because Mom and Dad always fight about where we should be and when we're supposed to come home." There was silence as Jennifer listened to her friend's response. "I don't care," she replied. "I just don't wanna hurt anybody's feelings. I just hate knowing Christmas is coming and they're gonna fight."

Tears welled in my eyes. I thought of our Christmas traditions—getting up before dawn, emptying the stockings as slowly as possible so they lasted a long time, opening one present, then watching as someone else opens theirs, cleaning up the trash, playing with new toys, trying on new clothes, and lounging in our jammies until it was time to drive to Aunt Suzy's for dinner. My heart broke, though, as I heard my daughter's description of another tradition: listening to parents fight. A court order gave me the girls on Christmas Day but at that moment I realized winning specific hours or special days wasn't important. The twins mattered most. I vowed to do whatever was necessary to stop the tradition of fighting. Right then, I chose to start a new tradition: peace. For their benefit, I let the girls stay with their father through Christmas morning. We would have the afternoon with my side of the family. I realized with a thankful heart that we had nearly every day of the year together; that I had the privilege of seeing the everyday miracles of their lives.

That's not to say that was the end of Christmas disputes. One year my ex-husband asked what gifts I got the twins for Christmas, then went out and bought exactly the same thing and gave it to them first on Christmas Eve! I was furious! But now I knew not to vent in front of my daughters. Instead, I called my sisters. They helped me put things into perspective and encouraged me to keep my focus on the girls. I stayed busy, fixed up our house, carved out a social life with friends, discarded expectations of the old life and watched them begin to fade. I grew to love my single life and refused to wear the label of "victim." Like my young daughters, I, too, blossomed in self-confidence and assurance.

Even though I disliked my former husband, I loved my girls and took seriously God's call to "train up a child in the way [she] should go" (Proverbs 22:6 KJV). I believed they needed strong relationships with their father and his parents and I encouraged frequent contact between them all. On holidays—Valentine's Day, birthdays, Mother's Day, and Father's Day—I made sure the girls remembered them with visits and small gifts or cards because I wanted them to grow up loving and respecting their father and grandparents.

In a series of Christmas losses—fire, death, divorce—I learned how to let go and I learned how to hold on. Just as the fire burned away material things that I cherished, the divorce consumed much of my emotional inventory. I remember looking for clothes or dishes that had burned. For a long time after the divorce, it felt strange to be without things that once were a part of my life but were lost—my wedding ring, the word "Mrs." in front of my name, and the closeness marriage brings.

In the spring, I thought about the times we went mushroom hunting and how I loved to watch the wild flowers come up. In the summer and fall, I remembered riding horses and hiking in the woods. In the winter, I was reminded of decorating our first and second houses for the holidays. But I had to let go of "what used to be." Like Lot's wife, I left an unholy place and my constant turning to see the past was a dangerous exercise in questioning God's wisdom. In time, my bitterness subsided, the pain eased, and my ex-husband and I achieved an uneasy alliance.

I heard friends and ministers speak about the emotional and physical impairment of unbridled bitterness. I knew I didn't want to live that way even though it would have been easy. As happens in many divorce situations, my ex and his wife made more money, had a nicer house, and drove better cars, but the girls and I were rich. We learned that security is not found in accumulating things. We welcomed the Lord in our house and knew his care. Eventually, the three of us had the privilege of introducing the Lord to their paternal grandparents and enjoying once again each other's company. That made years of hostility and separation a small price to pay.

It seems like a different lifetime when I cried on Christmas Eves and watched valuable aspects of my life go up in smoke. But as the girls and I endured losses, visitation court hearings, and penny-pinching, our love for each other has grown stronger, our faith in God more secure. My early fears that divorce would make delinquents of my twins seem almost laughable now; those fears were long ago laid to rest. The girls are happy and healthy teens, and I am a happy, healthier mom. God kept his promise. What could have harmed us was turned to good. Out of the fire and divorce rose up two beautiful young ladies and a stronger, more confident woman.

Now, when Christmas rolls around, I think of all of life's wonderful gifts rather than tragedy or "what used to be." I think of the gifts of love, of God's goodness, of faith, and the greatest of all—a baby boy born in a manger, the embodiment of salvation, the hope of eternal life. And nothing, not fire or death or divorce, can take away that gift.

twelve

Gifts Worth Waiting For

After a brief wait in a rather stark, institutional-style waiting area, I was ushered into a small conference room and introduced to a woman I'll call Deborah. A pleasant woman in her mid-thirties, she was simply dressed in a blue chambray shirt and pants. Long curly blond hair, brightened by a few strands of silver, softly framed her oval face. Direct, clear blue eyes revealed both serenity and sorrow. As she told her story, her beautiful, manicured hands gestured in assurance and grace.

During my interview, a steady stream of interruptions allowed me to watch Deborah respond to questions with the authority and expertise of a corporate executive. I haven't met many women capable of balancing knowledgeable certitude with such kindness and calmness. I was impressed.

Deborah is clearly a capable woman yet totally reliant on the Lord. Her presence and her story communicate forgiveness, hope, and compassion. After our time together, I wondered, "When Christ told his followers to feed the hungry, give water to the thirsty, welcome strangers, clothe the naked, visit those in prison, take care of the orphans and widows, was he thinking of women like Deborah?"

DEBORAH'S STORY

*I*n the mountains of the South where I was raised, Christmas was always about family. Simple traditions, like cutting down a fresh tree, were important to us. Some years Christmas consisted of the tree and not much more than that. I remember the year my mom was given some sets of fancy new panties. She turned right around and gave them to my sister and me, and those were the only gifts we received that year. I learned early in my life that Christmas, more than anything, is about family.

Every year, regardless of how much or little there was to spread across the table, generations of aunts, uncles, brothers, sisters, and cousins gathered at my grandmother's house for Christmas dinner. My mom was the second daughter of eight kids, so when we got together it was a big group. When my grandmother died, the tradition continued at my mom's. All through my elementary and high school years, friends and relatives hung around our house. They still do! Everyone loved being with my mother. Besides, Mom makes the best chicken and dumplings.

I have good memories of Christmas, but I didn't know a *real* Christmas until my daughter, Megan, was born. Holding Megan was holding love in my hands; love was something I could touch.

My sister and I knew that our mom loved us, but she never said so. I don't think it's true that actions and gifts are enough for a child. At least to me they weren't enough. I wanted my daughter to hear and to know the words, "I love you."

When Megan was about three, we went to McDonald's a lot for lunch. We both really enjoyed it because I got to talk with other moms and she got to play with her little friends. I remember one particular time when we finished eating and I cleaned her sticky ice cream face and gave her a kiss. She ran off to play but kept coming back to the table just long enough to say, "I love you, Mommy." It didn't matter where we were, it was always the right time to say, "I love you." There's never a wrong time. I think a lot about those days. So much has changed. Megan still says, "You're my best friend. I love you, Mom," only now she writes it in a letter.

We've been separated for eight years now. Everything changed one March night when Megan was five and my son, Michael, was six weeks old. Wayne and I decided to take the kids to my favorite aunt and uncle's who lived just down the road from my parents. I was very close to them, so we often took the kids to visit. They were what you'd call typical mountain people, simple, hard-working folks, who left their doors unlocked and encouraged relatives and friends to drop in. They were also independent and opinionated, and really distrustful of banks, so much so they kept their money hidden in cookie jars and under mattresses.

As we pulled up in front of the house, Michael got real fussy and started to cry. Wayne decided to go on inside, but I stayed in the car to change the baby's diaper and calm him down. Megan stayed with me, and like a typical five-year-old, helped take care of her baby brother. Once Michael was happy and dry, Megan and I played with him for a minute. Suddenly, we heard a loud noise outside the car. That sound was familiar and it seemed strangely out of place. Puzzled, I told Megan, "Stay in the car with Michael for a minute. I'll be right back."

I walked into the house and couldn't believe my eyes. I stared at a sickening scene and tried to make sense of what I saw in front of me. I don't know how to describe the next few minutes. My aunt and uncle lay dead, obviously murdered. Wayne was just standing there. It was so horrible, I freaked out and started screaming, "What have you done?"

Reason and logic often escape a person in times of horror. For reasons I don't fully understand or can't even begin to explain, I tried to help cover up the crime. I did what I was told to do without question. If I could go back and change any part of my life, it would be those few minutes. I remember just trying to get the job done so I could get out of that house and run back to my babies in the car. I didn't know what else to do. Within a matter of hours, I discovered there were a lot of things I didn't know. I didn't know Wayne had a gun or a drug addiction. I didn't know he had planned to rob my dear aunt and uncle. I'll never know how his intention to steal turned into murder or how a scheme to take money took two lives. I didn't know that a trip to visit my relatives would change the rest of my life.

In the eyes of the law, the fact that I was in the car made me as guilty as if I had pulled the trigger. I am not guilty of robbery or murder, but I'm not totally innocent. I panicked and foolishly tried to hide the crime, which was a big mistake. But my biggest mistake came next. I ran. I fled the state. For a year, I left my beautiful five-year-old daughter and my six-week-old son, and hid, terrified of what might happen to me. When I returned, I was placed in a county facility just two miles from my mother's house, where Michael, who was just learning to walk, and Megan, who attended school half-days, were now living.

While my lawyers worked on my case, my daily routine centered around the two meals County was required to serve. Breakfast arrived about 7:00 in the morning and dinner came about 5:00. The sheriff and his wife who took care of me in the small community jail always said, "Good morning. Here's breakfast." Sometimes they would kindly add, "It's good today." I would mumble "Good morning" or not even say a word. I hated myself so deeply I couldn't speak. I just wanted to die to stop the hurt I caused my family, my children, and myself.

Scheduled visits from my children were the only reason to live through the week. On Fridays, Mom brought my daughter to see me for half a day, and every Sunday, right after church, she brought both kids for an hour of visitation. Other than my mom and my children, no one else visited me so I wasn't expecting the man who suddenly appeared in front of my cell. I was startled, too, because he looked like Captain Hook without the hat! He was a tall, bald man, with a patch over one eye and a middle that showed he enjoyed his momma's good cooking. I was surprised when he said, "Deborah, I've been following your case. I'm in jail ministry and I want to read the Bible to you, if you'll let me." I looked at him for a few moments before I said, "Well, all right, have a seat." We each sat down and I listened.

He told me God was about love; that knowing God was a love thing, not a "rules and regulation" thing. He visited me Tuesday nights from 7:30 to 9:30 P.M. for a couple of weeks before he finally asked, "Deborah, do you want a relationship with God?" I said, "Yes" and on April 21, at 9:03 P.M., I prayed to accept Christ. For the first time in my life, I felt total peace. I felt embraced and whole. The emptiness I felt inside was filled with forgiveness and love.

The first thing I did was tell Megan. I remembered our days at McDonald's and how wonderful it was to say and hear "I love you." I explained in words she could understand just how much God loved us and then asked her the question the pastor asked me: "Would you like to love God?" Like her mother, Megan said, "Yes." The first person I led to the Lord was my six-year-old daughter.

The next thing I did over the next few months was read my Bible twice, cover to cover. I had never even read two full chapters of the Bible before, but now I really loved the stories in the Old Testament and the stories of Jesus in the New Testament. After the second reading, I wanted to be baptized so badly. I dreamed of being taken out of my cell and down to a river so I could be immersed. But I never told anyone, not the pastor, not Megan, not the sheriff or his wife. No one. When charged with something like I'm charged with, you don't dream very much, and I didn't want my dream taken away.

After thirteen months in County, I received my verdict: "Life sentence." The sheriff phoned my mom to tell her I'd be sent to the state prison the very next day. My entire family came to say goodbye, and they videoed my attempt to be strong and happy in front of my kids. Actually, I felt nothing but fear as I had no idea what to expect in the future. And I panicked at the thought of becoming even more separated from my children.

Over the mountains, 137 miles away, I was instantly placed in "segregation," an isolated cell, for the required 48-hour medical quarantine. I cried the entire time. For weeks after I was released into the general population and placed in my 6' x 9' cell, I cried myself to sleep. Then, I decided "enough." It was time to get busy. I was going to be here for a long time so I'd better learn how to live in this community.

The first thing I did was join five women in a weekly Bible study. And like every other woman here, I was assigned a job. As a teacher's aid, I helped 25 women prepare for their GED. Many of them didn't have more than a third-grade education but all of them had children. I was amazed at how they had provided for their families or even survived out in the free world. As I heard their stories, I gained such respect for them all.

Helping those women and attending the Bible study inspired the hope that I might work in the chaplain's office. The chaplain already had two assistants, each serving life terms, so it didn't seem likely that there would be an opening for me any time soon! But I dreamed and prayed about it anyway. Then, after eight months, a message came from the chaplain asking me to drop by his office later that afternoon. I got permission and arrived promptly at 3:15. I'll never forget that appointment.

"Deborah," he said, "you aren't going to believe this, but it's on my heart to offer you the job for the assistant."

"I didn't even know you had an opening," I blurted out.

Both positions had opened up, proof that the Lord will answer our prayers if it's in his will and glorifies him. As the chaplain's assistant, it's my responsibility to meet all the new women when they are admitted. I invite them to Bible studies and services, answer their questions about visitation, and explain that our Freedom Chapel is a sanctuary, a place of quiet and worship. I assist the chaplain and volunteer chaplains, and help coordinate the activities of 250 volunteers involved in twenty-seven programs directed from our office. It's hard work, requiring every bit of energy I can give, but it's so rewarding.

A lot of women in here come off the streets and don't know how to take care of themselves. They don't know the basics of personal hygiene. Volunteer programs teach these ladies life skills and show them how to take better care of themselves, both physically and spiritually.

During my first year in the chapel, I don't know how many times I said, "Chaplain, I am praying that we get a counselor for our women." There are so many different needs among women who range from 17 to 72, and they all need a friend to talk to. When they come to me and ask, "Deborah, what should I do?" my answer usually is, "I don't know, but I can listen." The pregnant girls are so scared when they arrive here. And they're scared when they're sent to the hospital for delivery. Then they're sad when they're taken from the maternity ward in handcuffs and brought back here alone. So many of them say, "You can't imagine how difficult it is to be separated from your baby." I answer, "No, not at birth I can't. At least I had my son for the first six weeks of his life." When I tell them that, they know I've felt the same pain and we can continue talking. I want to live as a Christian in front of these women because we all have a lot in common, no matter the reason for being here. Sentenced for drugs or stealing, in for four years or life, we're all still away from family and home.

When I first arrived, we didn't have any daytime counselors; now we have four who come three days a week to counsel women who are terminally ill from cancer or AIDS, or who may lose custody of children. They teach classes on stress management and parenting skills. Now our women can receive confidential counseling for alcoholism, post-abortion syndrome, and grief and anger management.

In prison, you truly learn who you are. We're no longer identified by clothes, big cars, or large homes. When women arrive here, they're given the same thing: three bras, three pairs of underwear, three pairs of socks, a tube of toothpaste, one toothbrush, and a small bottle of shampoo. We're given four sets of uniforms but shoes and everything else has to be purchased either in the commissary or sent from home. We're given twelve tampons a month, and if more are needed, we have to buy them.

Unfortunately, everything is more expensive here. We pay an additional 2¢ handling charge for every stamp even though this is a federal facility. Phone companies have an agreement with the prison system so all our calls have to be collect. We can't use pre-paid calling cards. There's a $2.95 connecting fee and a per-minute rate of 22¢. Most families can't afford that so our calls home are infrequent and short.

The chaplain's assistant position pays fifty cents an hour or about $65 a month. I spend about $25 on basic personal items: soap, shampoo, combs, pens. The only way to survive is with the help of family and friends. It helps when they send stuff that is allowed: stamps, better bras, any white or gray clothing, sweats for winter and T-shirts for summer. The only color allowed in our wardrobe must be hidden beneath our uniforms, so we love green or purple socks and red panties! And we love getting stuff that brightens up our day, like cards for Valentine's Day and birthdays and special occasions. Little things, pictures and bookmarks, confetti and stickers are pleasant surprises.

Like citizens of any town, we exercise, read, work, shop, worship, exist. When people come in from the free world, we need to hear about the details of their lives. Nearly 80 percent of us will go back out so we need to hear the truth about real life. We say to the volunteers, "Tell us if your husband or your kids woke up cranky, the check got lost in the mail, and your electricity is about to be turned off. Complain about bad traffic and leaky roofs. We forget about so many things in the free world." It's not easy for women when they are released. There's only a handful out of the 540 women here who *don't* consider themselves second-class citizens. It's hard to have dignity and confidence when being judged and condemned after you've done your time. When we're released, it's time for a second chance.

As the chaplain's assistant, I try to help women prepare for whatever future they face. I want to treat each one with respect, without judgment. I want them to know about the Lord, so I try to know about them. One woman arrived on December 25, Christmas Day, and was placed in the required isolation. Within hours, notes had been slipped to her, proposals from the "men" in the prison asking for dates. When the door opened for her release into the general population, I was standing there. I wanted to be the first person she saw. I wanted my voice to be the first one she heard. I wanted God's love in me to be the first friendship she experienced. So I waited outside her door.

When she stepped out, she had the look in her eyes and expression on her face that clearly said, "If you say the wrong thing to me, I'm gonna deck you." I looked straight into her eyes, and said, "Hello. I'd like to introduce myself. My name is Deborah. Do you have a Bible?"

Her eyes got really big and she shook her head, "No." That meeting was the beginning of our friendship. As a matter of fact, she became my prayer partner and we've been in the same Bible study for six years now. The study I first attended with five other women right after I arrived has grown to 65. Actually, more than 180 of our women attend five separate Bible studies during the week.

I love how much things have grown and changed here— including me. I was here for months before I realized that my old dream could come true. I could be baptized. Freedom Chapel has a small mobile baptismal about the size of a small table top. I'll never forget the day I stepped down into the water and sat on the built-in seat, the minister stood on the outside and reached over the edge to immerse me. I went under that water believing the death of Jesus was for me and came up knowing the thick sense of sin I lived with for so long was washed away—all of it. It was a great day of cleansing for me, one I want every woman here to experience.

My job in the chapel allows me to take part in every woman's baptism. My responsibility is to fill the pool and empty it, and I do it with joy in my heart. Some women say, "I can't believe you do a job like that," but it's a privilege for me. Baptism is in remembrance of our Lord and brings us closer to him, and it's one of the few ways we can openly show our peers we are proud God is in our lives.

The only thing I love more than sharing in baptisms is when my children come to visit. Since my family lives so far away, they usually make the trip only one day a month. For the first hour they're here, the kids compete for my attention. They both talk non-stop and fuss with each other between races back and forth to the vending machines for junk food. Visitors are not allowed to bring in gifts or personal items, just $10 worth of change, so I let my kids buy anything they want to eat. I don't care about sugar rushes. If they are eating, they're hungry. If they're hungry, they have an appetite. If they have an appetite, they're healthy. We celebrate our birthdays with a cupcake and use a pretzel for a candle. I can't give them any presents while they're here, except processed food and my undivided attention.

Megan always sits on my left, links her arm through mine and snuggles up close enough to whisper in my ear. Teenagers. What do they do? They keep secrets. So Megan wants to be close enough to tell me her secrets. Michael sits on my right side so we can play games. I use my right hand to draw or play checkers with him. Megan tugs on my left arm to let me know I'm not listening to her closely enough. But I'm always listening. I'm so blessed by their visits.

When we're together, we try to fill in what got left out of our weekly letters. I even play tic-tac-toe with Michael through the mail. He makes a mark and sends it to me, I make a mark and send it to him. The game can last for weeks, but that's OK. When he was little and was learning his alphabet, I made the letters out of dots so he could connect them to form his letters. He'd send them back so I could see how well he was learning to write. Once my daughter had to make a globe out of a pumpkin. She coated the outside blue and then painted on the shapes of the continents. I called home with a few suggestions and ideas. My family has been really good about letting me stay involved in their academic life. I pictured in my mind Michael sitting at the table tracing his letters and Megan hollowing out her pumpkin to make her globe. Imagination is such a sweet gift from God.

I am blessed that my kids are so open with me. They have asked every question imaginable, from sex to why I'm here. Sometimes we moms think, "Our children know all that. Why bother talking about sex—they've seen it on TV." We think, "I'm not going there." But we do need to go there. And if anyone deserves to know why we are here, it is definitely our children. We have to prepare them for the future and tell them the truth about everything. We can't be in this situation and not be honest with our kids. They deserve better than that. They deserve our honesty and more.

The most difficult time for me and for any mother in prison is when a child asks when we're coming home. Once Michael asked, "If I went in there and said, 'Please, please, please,' three times, would they let you out?" I had to look my baby in the face and say, "No." Some things never get easy. But I hold onto the biblical truth that what was meant to harm me, God turned to good. My kids and I watch God link everything together for good.

Of the few photographs I have of my kids, my favorite one of Megan shows her standing beside her friend Kelly. They're in matching white robes, hugging each other just a few minutes before their baptisms. Megan and Kelly became good friends after Kelly nonchalantly mentioned that she didn't live with her mom. Megan softly answered, "Me, too." They found a common bond and forged a friendship and sealed it in baptism.

For the first time since I've been here, last Christmas fell on Saturday, a visitation day. I knew my mom was planning to bring the kids and I asked, "What time are you all going to get here?" She said, "If I get the kids up early to open their gifts, we should be up there by 9:30 or 10:00."

"That's good," I told her, "We have four women who want to be baptized on Christmas Day. I'll get the baptismal filled up first, then I'll go down to the visitation lobby. I'll be waiting." My daughter knew they were coming but my son didn't. They didn't want him to be disappointed if snow or bad weather made them cancel the trip.

They were so excited, they woke up around 4:30 in the morning and opened their gifts while my mom took pictures. And that was a gift to me! The one thing my Mom's usually not good about is taking pictures on holidays and birthdays, but this Christmas, my kids were captured on film. I have a new favorite picture of Michael, grinning ear to ear, snapped just as he jumped on his new bicycle. After all the presents were opened and enjoyed for a while, Michael was told to get dressed.

"Why?" he asked. "So we can go see your mom." He let out a whoop and yelled, "What?! We're going to see Mom?" and took off to get ready.

The tradition in our family is that gifts to relatives and special friends are placed under the tree before Christmas, but nothing for our immediate family. Megan and Michael write their letters to Santa in early December and put them under the tree. They change the list several times before Christmas Eve, when Santa reads the letters, eats his cookies, and leaves the requested things. This year, Mom told me that Michael had five things on his list to Santa. Number one: a new bike. Number five: Please bring Mom home. I couldn't go home, but because it was a Saturday, he could come here and spend Christmas Day with me.

I was waiting for them when they got here. Michael immediately started telling about the gifts he opened. But not just gifts from Santa. "Mom, I got this sweater from Fairview! And I got a bike from Jane in Westville." Women I work with, volunteers who are like family to me, sent gifts to my children on my behalf. Unopened packages with unknown names and addresses stacked up under the tree, next to Michael and Megan's letters to Santa. Apparently Michael read the names *and* the return address on them because it was important for him to know the name of the city as well. The excitement in his voice, the smile on his face, and his happiness with his gifts are what I've missed through all the Christmases of his life.

I was reminded again that Christmas is about family. Not just blood family, but one made by people in my community and the volunteers I work with. Michael and Megan's growing sense of family now include people they don't personally know who live in cities they've never visited. This year, my best Christmas gifts were not sent through the mail or wrapped in paper. They were the generosity of God's family and the presence of Megan and Michael. And the four baptisms.

Life's most precious gifts come from unexpected sources, even the Bible. Being separated from my children is nearly unbearable and often the only comfort I find is in Scripture. Not long after Christmas, one night in chapel, I was reading the tenth chapter of Hebrews. When I got to verses 12 and 13, my mouth fell open. "But when Christ had offered for all time a single sacrifice for sins, he sat down at the right hand of God, and since then has been waiting..." (NRSV). I stopped reading right there. Waiting. Christ understands waiting. He knows what it means to wait.

I literally went weak in the knees and fell to the floor. "Oh, God," I prayed. "Thank you for letting me see that you wait." My life is all about waiting. I wait for my children to visit; I wait for women to come out of segregation. I wait for my meals and for the doors to open so I can begin my day in the chaplain's office. I wait for the mail to be delivered, I wait for the volunteers to arrive and help the ladies here. I wait for the Lord to teach me to wait on him because he always answers. And I wait for him to come back for us soon.

My body may be confined, but my spirit is free. I have freedom in Christ. But I wait for the day when my body is set free and I can watch my children sleep. I wait for the time we eat a healthy meal around a family table and attend a Christmas Eve church service together. I wait for the time when we will celebrate birthdays with a big cake and real candles. I wait to be included in family pictures. I wait...

In the meantime, I wait for the ladies in my community to accept the Lord, while He waits for them too.

thirteen

The Gift of a Name

Grace wears a burgundy velvet blouse fastened at the collar with a large turquoise pendant. A silver squash-blossom necklace drapes to her waist. Her once long black hair, now short and white as snow, waves around her softly lined face. Slightly stooped with age, she still walks with the aura of a strong, regal woman.

Aided by her daughters, Dorothy and Cookie, Grace tells the story of her life as a Native American daughter, celebrating Christmases before her family knew of sewing machines, before cars replaced horses, before electricity replaced fire, before houses were built alongside hogans.

Grace, a 96-year-old wise Navajo, lives with her daughters in Window Rock, Arizona, the matriarch of a legacy of faith.

GRACE'S STORY

*L*ineage in the Navajo tribe is traced through the mother. Around 1864, my great-grandmother joined other women and warriors for the "Long Walk." Under the direction of Kit Carson, Navajo walked hundreds of miles into forced captivity. They were told they were being taken to Fort Sumner for their safety, but many were tortured and abandoned along the way. The weak were left beside the trail to die of starvation. Our sheep herds were left behind to die, our crops were burned, our peach trees were deliberately destroyed to discourage resettling. Before the Long Walk, great-grandmother had never had contact with the white people.

At Fort Sumner, she married an Irish soldier and went with him when he was transferred to Fort Defiance. Three years later, my grandmother was born. When the captain returned to his home in the east, my great-grandmother refused to move with him. She took her two children and walked with the Navajo survivors back to the homeland.

My grandmother and my mother both married Navajos and the Irish blood died out. In 1904, when my mother was only 13, I was born in the desert by the Colorado River, near Winslow,

Arizona. Among Navajo, it is the common practice for maternal aunts or grandmothers to name girl children while boys are named by men during a religious ceremony. On the second day of my life, my grandmother pierced my ears and gave me the birth name of Biłagibah. I was called "Bah" which means "war." The Navajo were in conflict quite a bit of the time and names often related to warfare.

When I was seven, my family settled by the Little Colorado River, across the wash from a Presbyterian mission school named Tolcheco. In 1912, I was sent there for the entire nine-month term and only came home for three months in the summer. I was the only one in my family to go to school. My younger brother and sister looked up to me as I told them about the things I did and learned at Tolcheco.

The missionaries made students wear white man's clothes and gave each one a Christian name. I happened to be named after a woman who took care of the boys at school—"Grace." But when I went home I was still called "Bah" and wore my native velvet blouse and long cotton skirt. My aunts handmade the broomstick pleats with six yards of material in each skirt. No sewing machines.

There were about 25 Navajo children at the mission. We were supposed to talk English all day long, which was strange and difficult to us, so some rarely spoke. But in the evening, after supper and before bed, we could talk Navajo all we wanted. We remembered what we did in the hogan and how it was different from the white man's ways. In the hogan we slept on sheepskins on the ground; at school we slept on cots covered with sheets. At home, our usual food was ground corn made into bread; now we ate things like lettuce and fresh vegetables. I never felt homesick; living here was better than at home.

When I was a girl in my hogan, adults would say, "Don't do this, don't say that, don't think about it…or the spirits will come and get you." Just scary threats without any explanation. We didn't talk about spirits, and I didn't know much about them except I knew they frightened me. At Tolcheco, the missionaries taught us about a God who loved us and wanted to take care of us. They explained that God loved us enough to send down his own Son.

I had never really known or felt love before, so when I heard about God's love, I just accepted it and the hogan life left me. I took the Lord into my heart at age seven and never let go. I guess I didn't show it much until I was twelve years old, when I was baptized in the horses' water trough. I lived at Tolcheco until 1919 and dreamed of becoming a missionary.

After my last summer vacation from school, as part of my education I was sent to Flagstaff to live with a western family. I was a full-time housekeeper, taught to clean, prepare meals, and do laundry for a dollar a week. I liked the work and was glad to get out of the hardship at home. After a few years, my mother wanted me to return to the hogan and learn Navajo ways. She wanted me to learn to raise children, to weave, and to cook traditional food.

For a year and a half, I lived with my mother and brother and sister and stepfather. I sometimes stayed up late at night grinding corn for the next day. I held a rock shaped like a loaf of bread in both hands and ground the corn against the matate stone on the floor. It was tedious and tiring, traditional girls' work. It had to be done so the family could eat.

My brother and sister and I learned to herd my mother's 150 sheep. It was up to us to stay with them all day long. I learned how to shear them and deliver lambs. I loved the long days in the sunshine, sitting next to the sheep, watching them graze, keeping them safe from snakes and coyotes. Sometimes I would sit in the shade of a tree and pray to Jesus. I prayed for the salvation of my family and for God to lead me in the way of his will. I believed in prayer.

Our hogan and grazing land were on top of the Coconinos, north of Flagstaff. I was 17 years old when my stepfather asked my mother for me as his second wife. Our custom allowed that, but I didn't want to be a second wife to anybody. In the dead of winter, I climbed through drifts of snow to the top of Gray Mountain. I prayed and prayed that someone would deliver me. God knew what had been done, what had been said; he knew everything. So I just asked to be taken from there.

Two days later, around noon, two men on horseback rode toward my brother who was herding sheep. One man spoke English and the other was his interpreter. They asked for me. My brother told them I was in the hogan and that I could talk English. They came inside and Reverend Trevor asked if I wanted to go to school and become an interpreter. I immediately said yes.

That night, the men slept outside in their bedrolls. Early the next morning, I gathered my things, then rode on horseback 50 miles through the snow and ice to the government school in Tuba, Arizona. I never looked back.

Reverend Trevor was a stranger to me, and I didn't know how he knew I wanted to get out of the hogan. I didn't write anyone or tell anyone other than God. I didn't know where to go to get help until the day I climbed Gray Mountain and could see Navajo land for miles, where I told God I wanted to go back to school. God answered my prayer. That's how strong prayer is.

From the government school, I went to the Ganado Mission School and finished the eighth grade. That's where I met Roger, my future husband. He had grown up near Fort Defiance and his father was a great medicine man who had learned all the chants and prayers from his father-in-law. He wanted Roger educated in the white man's ways and chose the Protestant mission rather than the Catholic "long coats." Later, he respected the beliefs of his Christian son, but rejected Jesus as his personal savior. He said when he prayed, it was to the same God that Christians prayed to.

After a few years in school, Roger got sick with tuberculosis and was sent to a sanitarium in Phoenix. After a year of treatment, the TB was so far advanced they sent him back to his hogan in Wheatfield to die. A white missionary heard that Roger understood English well enough to interpret, so he went out and invited Roger to go with him to the mission in Chinle. The missionary's wife nursed him back to health, allowing him to get out of bed only on Sunday mornings to interpret.

Somehow Roger heard about me in Ganado and came courting. He was not tall, but he was handsome! Even as a young man, he had a commanding presence. Roger was a devout Christian, good with words, both Navajo and English. He was very wise and I couldn't help falling in love with him. He rode the 40 miles from Chinle to Ganado on horseback at least twice a month to court me. We also wrote letters to each other for three years before he asked me to be his cook. We were married in 1925 in front of Roger's family. My family could not come because it was too far away and they only had one donkey. The missionaries helped arrange our Christian wedding, and one of the ladies made my white Chinese silk dress and veil. It had a drop waist and a big bow at the skirt, in the style of the 1920s. I still have the dress. In fact, I just gave it to my fourteen-year-old great-granddaughter so she can wear it when she grows up and gets married.

In our first job in Chinle, Roger was paid $50 a month as interpreter for Reverend Charles Byseggar at a mission church. Reverend Byseggar would say a sentence or read from the Bible and Roger would interpret into Navajo. They did this on Sunday mornings in church and every day during home visitations. They'd go into hogans and ask how the family was doing and talk about other things. Then they'd talk about the Bible for as long as people wanted to hear. We were in Chinle for twelve years. I stayed at home and took care of our children in the little two-bedroom rock house we built close to the missionary's home.

Christmas drew the biggest crowds to the church. Hogans were all spread out, so when the Navajo came in to the trading post, they would hear about the Christmas program. Then, they'd ride from hogan to hogan and spread the news. Some of the Christian families who came to church would invite other Navajos. That's how word got out.

About 500–600 Navajo would show up for the Christmas program. Before it started, we handed out little gifts, like clothes, combs, or toys to each one and fed them mutton stew. They stayed for the service, but they mostly came to make their stomachs happy. They'd leave with full stomachs and gifts, but very few took the story of Jesus' birth with them when they left. Just like now, people go to church on Christmas Eve for entertainment or tradition and leave without taking Jesus with them.

In 1936, the Presbytery sent us to Indian Wells, near Holbrook, on the southern edge of the reservation. We were the first natives to run a mission without a western man's supervision and we turned an empty hospital building into a church. The Navajo turned their backs on us for a while, but later they knew we were true talkers. Some people didn't speak the truth, but they trusted our words.

The next year, we got a black Chevy sedan from the mission board. Roger and I worked hard to tell our people about the Lord. At first, when they heard our car coming, the men would leave the hogan and the women would turn their backs and start doing something, like weaving or carding or spinning, and ignore us. But it wasn't very long before they were so glad to see us, the coffee-pot would be at the fire and they'd all gather for a little meeting with us. Sometimes they'd feed us.

During this time, all five of our children attended the Rehoboth Mission in New Mexico, near Gallup, about 140 miles away. Just like I had done in Tolcheco, they lived there for nine months and only came home for the summer. During the war, gas was rationed and we couldn't visit the kids except at Christmas. But when they were home with Roger and me, we sang together every morning before family devotions. We raised the roof! I played the piano, two daughters sang soprano, one sang alto, our sons sang tenor, and Roger sang bass. We sang choruses like "Heavenly Sunshine" and "Jesus Loves Me." My daughter Dorothy always wanted to sing "In the Cross I Glory" and Cookie wanted to sing "O Happy Day." Roger's favorite hymn was "Rock of Ages." I loved the Navajo and English versions of "In the Garden."

Our church had a membership of maybe 30 to 40 elderly people. The young people weren't as accepting. The ones who came wanted friendship, not knowledge about God. The Navajo ask, "What's the use of being a Christian? Look at this one; he was a Christian and taught the Bible. Now he goes out and drinks." Alcoholism is the main reason for hardship and illness among the Navajo. It breaks my heart.

The Navajo people have a hard time loving God and believing in his Son. They don't want to talk about the Lord Jesus dying on the cross or taking him to the grave because they don't like to hear or think about death. When someone died, they came to us and said, "There's a body out there." Roger and I would have to get the body, bring it back to the mission, and bury it. They wouldn't touch or help wash the body. When a person dies, Navajo custom is to wrap them up and bury them the same day. The ones who carry the body, or wrap it up, are unclean for four days. They stay to themselves until the fourth morning when they have a cleansing ceremony; they wash their body and their hair before they can join the others.

We finally got the Navajo to the place where they'd come in for a service to honor the person who died. At first, they wouldn't come at all. But later it got so that they'd come for a service and even help prepare the body. Then the family mourned privately. Even though I am Navajo, I never got used to the custom for a dead child. The baby was put outside, away from the hogan, and left without anyone watching it. That got me at first. It's like they didn't care what happened to it, but to them, the child was dead. What else could be done?

I've seen native funeral ceremonies on television where there's a big fire and singing and dancing. That's not true for the Navajo. They believe when a person dies, their spirit lingers for four days before leaving. That person's name is never spoken again. The Navajo are afraid if they speak the person's name, the spirit will come back. Even the dead man's horse is killed near the grave site. His saddle and all his belongings are placed in the grave, not because the person needs his possessions for his next journey, they just want to forget about the dead person. They don't want to see any reminders. Recently a clan brother of mine died of cancer. They didn't shoot his horse; they put a needle in him. My brother's saddle and all of his things were put down in the grave with him. That's sad.

Roger was on the Navajo Council for 28 years, from 1936 until he died in 1964. Council delegates from each area of the reservation met in Window Rock to make new laws and attend to Navajo business. Some of the men were missionaries, like Roger. After Roger's death, I served his last two years in the Council and then gave it over to somebody else. I wanted to carry on with our church work.

Until 1970, I continued at the mission and attended all the women's meetings and conferences in the Arizona Presbytery. I held Sunday services and Wednesday night prayer meetings, and met with people who came to visit. I drove out to the day schools and gave religious instruction to the students. Even now, a lot of them come up to me and say, "We remember what you said."

I mentioned that the Navajo came to Christmas programs even when they wouldn't come to a regular church service. One year, an elderly man and his wife played the roles of Joseph and Mary. I was in charge of the evening, but first I had to go pick up some people who lived out in the hills, about 10 miles from the mission. My truck got stuck in the sand and I didn't make it back in time for the service. Later, I learned that everyone in the church had waited and waited for me. When it was obvious that I wasn't going to show up, the man portraying Joseph stood up and told the Christmas story. They didn't do the pageant with the shepherds and wise men. He just told the story. Maybe that was a good thing. Navajo are storytelling people and he told the simple story of the birth of Jesus. I wish I could have heard him.

I have no regrets for my life, except one. I wish more Navajo loved God. Too many of them are now a part of the Native American Church, just so they can smoke peyote. The people have left practicing Navajo ways and have adopted Plains Indian activities and culture. Peyote is a drug from cactus, and alcohol came from the white culture. Both of these things are hurting the Navajo. My people accept those bad things but they won't accept that God loves everyone. But that doesn't stop me from doing the Lord's work.

Some Navajo did accept the truth of God. I was so blessed when my own mother finally gave herself to the Lord. For years, I prayed for her and with her. My brother doesn't have any use for Christianity. He's old now and still rejects it. All of my children believe and my oldest son is a pastor. My younger son is thinking about becoming a missionary after he retires. He's only sixty. But the younger generations do not believe. They struggle with alcoholism and that hurts me. I pray for them because I know God answers prayer.

I'm 96 but I still feel young. I am the last living student from the Tolcheco school. I make my own breakfast—but I don't have to grind corn anymore! My life has been a good long walk, not the forced walk of my great-grandmother. My name was changed from Biłagibah to Grace and my heart went from war to peace. My soul threw out the fear of spirits and took in the loving Spirit of God. I am Navajo, I am Christian, and I am an example of what God's grace can do for anyone who loves him.

Mary's Song

Blue homespun and the bend of my breast
keep warm this small hot naked star
fallen to my arms. (Rest...
you who have had so far
to come.) Now nearness satisfies
the body of God sweetly. Quiet he lies
whose vigor hurled
a universe. He sleeps
whose eyelids have not closed before.
His breath (so slight it seems
no breath at all) once ruffled the dark deeps
to sprout a world.
Charmed by doves' voices, the whisper of straw,
he dreams,
hearing no music from his other spheres.
Breath, mouth, ears, eyes
he is curtailed
who overflowed all skies,
all years.
Older than eternity, now he
is new. Now native to earth as I am, nailed
to my poor planet, caught that I might be free,
blind in my womb to know my darkness ended,
brought to this birth
for me to be newborn,
and for him to see me mended
I must see him torn.

—Luci Shaw

fourteen

Only God Could Think of This

Georgalyn Wilkinson is an accomplished woman with an impressive collection of titles: preacher's daughter, missionary kid, college graduate, young bride, missionary wife, public speaker, mother, and international radio host.

Those who know her well describe her not as a paradox but paradoxically. Georgalyn is both the velvet pouch and the fiery faceted diamond inside. She is a feminine powerhouse determined to tell the world of God's paradox: The Creator of the universe came to the earth as a child in a manger.

Softness and strength, gentle laughter and deep compassion describe this woman, who after twenty-seven years with the Far East Broadcasting Company now serves as President of Gospel Literature International in Ontario, California. Oh, yes—she saved her favorite title for last: proud grandmother.

GEORGALYN'S STORY

*W*henever I am asked "Where are you from?" I never quite know how to answer. I was born in Ohio, but lived there for only a few years before my father took a pastorate in Virginia. Then we lived in Florida and Alabama before my dad moved our family to the Philippines where he worked with the Far East Broadcasting Company (FEBC).

I was sixteen and a high school graduate when we arrived in Manila, and very quickly I was asked to help my parents and other career missionaries in the radio ministry. I learned to do a variety of jobs, never knowing that down the road I would hire people to do the very same work I learned as a teenager. The Lord prepared me well for my future.

I was eighteen when I returned to the United States to attend college in South Carolina. There I met a blue-eyed, curly-headed blond man named David. He was a radio and television production major and had already applied to FEBC for full-time mission work. He seemed excited to meet me because he had heard that I had first-hand knowledge about FEBC and intended to work for them after college. During our time together, we enjoyed the mesh of our interests and goals and soon realized we had fallen deeply in love. Two weeks after our graduations we married, packed our few belongings, and flew to Okinawa for our first overseas assignment.

David was program director for three FEBC radio stations, each beaming out in a different language: Japanese for the Okinawans, Chinese to mainland China, and English for the US military personnel and their families living on the island. David and I hosted a two-hour program every morning called *Sunny Side Up*. We were nicknamed "The Two Fried Eggs" and our "menu" included American sports reports, the time and weather, and up-to-the-minute news. We bantered easily on the air together, telling silly jokes, teasing the chaplains who we predicted would most likely parachute into a rice paddy, and reminding troops of home and their Christian backgrounds. Many servicemen said our program helped them stay faithful, both to home and to the Lord. Those were rewarding, wonderful years.

Four years on Okinawa passed quickly when, as if a love gift from God, we learned we were expecting our first child. When our daughter was born we combined her grandmother's maiden name with the Japanese word for rose, which gave our daughter both a family name and a Japanese name: Barra. We loved her name and we loved her.

Shortly after Barra's birth, we returned to the States for a year of furlough. Then we packed again for a move to Tokyo, where David served as the field director of FEBC. Our time in Okinawa was like living in the country, but living in the mega-city of Tokyo required several levels of adjustment for us, most especially for me.

We had barely finished unpacking before we faced the realization that the Japanese culture prevented my active involvement so familiar in our style of ministry. In Japan, a man in a responsible position does not work with his wife. She doesn't accompany him to business meetings and she certainly isn't identified with any part of his work. I understood this cultural difference, but I couldn't imagine that it would apply to me! David and I had worked together all the years of our marriage. I had been a part of

FEBC since my teens. Now I was expected to relinquish the abilities God gave me in administration and script writing and contact with people through on-the-air programming. Working with FEBC was also my calling, my ministry, not just David's.

One day, alone with the Lord, I asked him to help me be willing to separate from the daily radio work. Yet, deep down, I didn't want to pray that prayer. I knew I could stay away from the office, but I also knew that if God didn't change the deep desires of my heart, I would just be pretending it was fine. I sincerely wanted to be a loving, supportive wife; I wanted to give David the freedom to do his job without concerns about my attitude. That was my prayer.

It didn't take long before the answer was literally in front of me! To my surprise, I was expecting our second child. Unlike my uneventful pregnancy with Barra, this time I was very, very sick. Each day I grew weaker due to severe anemia. As foreign missionaries in Japan, we had access to the Seventh-Day Adventist clinic, but getting there required a three-hour round trip journey by bus and train. Every other day, two-year-old Barra and I made the trip to the clinic for my Vitamin B shots and a doctor's visit. One day on the ride home, lulled by the rhythm of the swaying train, I thought, *What if I were still working in the FEBC office every day?* If I had been actively involved, people would be scrambling to take on the additional responsibilities of my work. Now, no one was inconvenienced and I wasn't letting anyone down by being absent. What a wonderful relief that was to my heart. Once again, God was ahead of me.

Our second daughter was born in April, 1965, and named Janel for her grandmothers Janet and Marvel. For the next six years, I happily raised our girls and loved the privilege of being a full-time mom. David stayed busy with the radio ministry and a heavy schedule of international travel. He honored our partnership by privately keeping me informed and seeking my counsel while honoring the Japanese custom of keeping his public work among men. I was not completely "out" of the field I loved, but in no way was I officially "in."

One sunny August day of 1971, I answered a phone call that forever changed my life. David, on a business trip to Korea, had collapsed in his room and was unconscious. He was obviously in critical condition and no one there knew what to do. He was unable to speak, and the attending Korean doctors knew nothing of his medical history. I needed to get to him quickly. Two terrifying hours later, with only my pocketbook on my arm, I boarded a flight to Seoul. Five hours later, I stood beside the pale, still body of my husband. All that we would ever say to each other had been said. Within 48 hours, without ever regaining consciousness, David died, felled as he worked in a job he loved from the unknown presence of a deeply imbedded brain tumor.

I can't imagine experiencing a greater moment of loneliness than when I stood in the stillness of an unfamiliar Korean hospital. I quietly wept. I was in a foreign country and didn't speak the language. I didn't know a single woman there, didn't know where the American Embassy was, and certainly didn't know how to find a morgue. I felt utterly helpless. I look back now and treasure that time when I was without a crutch, without my pastor, without my parents, without my children or a friend. In those moments, I was *not* without the presence of God. It was God and me. Alone. Together.

I remember praying, "Lord, you could have healed him, but you didn't, and he's gone. I'm only 36 years old with two small children and now I'm a widow." Then I remember saying to him, "All right, Lord, since you have allowed this, I want to be the neatest widow you've ever made. I want to accept this from your heart and bring you great honor." I'm sure I was in shock, but I somehow accepted this from the depth of my being. Totally. Without question. Ever!

The US military came to my aid and flew David's body back to Japan. I will always be proud of the magnificent way they reached out to one of their citizens. David was buried in the International

Cemetery in Yokohama on a dark, rainy summer day. My heart mirrored the weather, but underlying all the grief was a definite and sure peace.

So much change followed David's death. So many decisions had to be made. Janel started to school on the Monday following David's funeral on Thursday. I remember that morning with such clarity, standing at the door, watching her follow Barra to the front gate of our compound. Janel and I had visited her school a few weeks earlier to check out the first-grade classroom and greet her teacher. Since parents were not encouraged to accompany children on the first day of school, I put on a brave "Mom" face as the girls set out for school with two other missionary children from our compound.

In what soon became their daily routine, these four little ones left their houses, walked to the bus stop, took the bus to the train station, walked under the station to the front side, climbed up the stairs to an elevated platform, waited for the correct train, and boarded it for a one-hour ride. When they got off the train, they skipped along the edge of a rice paddy and walked across a field to reach their school. Barra had done this routine well for two years, and I knew that her little sister would be fine with her. But that morning when I kissed my blond-headed baby and sent her off with a pat on her soft ringlet curls, my tears held fear as well as joy.

I waved goodbye as my girls joined the two children from next door. Just then, their father came out of their house and spoke to Janel. I couldn't hear what he said, but I watched him reach down and give her a swift pat on her bottom as he whispered something in her ear. Later he told me he had asked, "Nel, are you ready for school today?" He noticed her quivering lower lip as she put her head down. At that point, he reached down and gave her a little swat. "Get going, young lady. You'll be fine." She straightened up and marched out of there just like a little trooper. Of course, I wept again when I heard what happened. At that moment, it was as if God was saying to me, "I will always add the proper masculine dimension to your children's lives." I was assured that a father figure would always influence their development.

I wasn't sure what the immediate future held for me. At first I thought that our little family of three should return to the States. Never did I think of replacing David, not in a country where women are not allowed to lead. But unknown to me, national staff and those in FEBC's headquarters in the US had conferred and soon asked me to stay as their ministry leader. After several weeks I agreed to assume David's position. Instead of calling me Director, they gave me the title of Directrix. For the next eight years, my peers lovingly addressed me by a new nickname: Trixie.

The Japanese summer cooled into fall and the change of seasons reminded me that Christmas was coming—our first Christmas without Daddy. I longed to be with my parents in Manila for the holidays, but no matter how I totaled the finances, I couldn't afford the flight. I found myself more and more preoccupied with thoughts of having to manage this first Christmas without my husband and without my family. Opening the mail one day, I was delighted to see the return address of dear friends in the States. My mouth dropped open when I read, "It would be so wonderful if you could visit your parents over Christmas. We want you and the girls to go—if you can get away. Let us know how much it will cost and we'll send a check." I was floored! Their sensitive hearts knew just what we three girls needed.

I hurriedly made arrangements to be away and purchased plane tickets for a December 24 flight on Philippine Airlines. How happy I was to be going home to Manila, to my parents, to the place I had fallen in love with FEBC and radio ministry. On Christmas Eve, the girls and I excitedly boarded the jumbo jet. We were going to Grandma and Grandpa's to be loved, hugged, and downright spoiled. About midway into the flight, I felt Janel squirming beside me. "What are you doing, Nel?" I asked. She turned away from me. "Janel, what's the matter? Are you sick?" Then I saw that she wasn't ill, she was trembling, trying to hide her sobs. Tears streamed down her little face. "Janel," I asked, "honey, what is it?" She couldn't answer. Finally, she blurted out, "He won't know where I am." Confused, I asked, "He what?"

"Santa," she said. "He will never find me. He doesn't even know where I'm going." Suddenly I realized: It's Christmas Eve, we're up here going to some faraway place and she must think that we'll have no Christmas at all. No celebration or tree or presents. What *else* could be taken from this tender little Nel! I pulled her close and said, "Honey, he will find us, believe me, he will." But inside I was thinking, "What can I do for this child?" I looked over at Barra sitting beside Janel, her little face stiff with worry. I could see that she wasn't sure that her little sister wasn't right. I sat beside my two girls, one quietly sobbing and the other quietly anxious. I was moved by their attempt to keep their fears to themselves, not wanting to add to my grief, not wanting to hurt me. We were, after all, facing our first Christmas without the Daddy who was so much a loving part of our lives, and we wanted to do all we could to ease each other's pain. There was little I could do except put my arms around them both in an effort to console them.

A few moments later, a flight attendant stopped beside my aisle seat. "Excuse me, ma'am," he said. "The pilot has requested a visit with these two sweet young ladies. Would you allow them to come with me into the cockpit?"

I thought to myself, "Oh dear. You don't know it, but this isn't the best time. There are real tears here." But I turned and asked the girls if they would like to go. They both sniffed and nodded yes. I quickly wiped Janel's face and moved to let them out of their seats. I watched as they hesitantly took the attendant's hands and walked toward the cockpit.

Alone in my seat I prayed, "Oh, Lord, what am I supposed to do? I thought this trip was so right. Am I really going to make it as a single parent? Like right now, I'm not sure how to handle this one all alone." I asked the Lord for wisdom, for words to comfort my daughters, and for strength to survive in this new and foreign land of widowhood.

A little while later, the cockpit door flew open and Janel came bounding out. Just a few steps ahead of her big sister, she marched down the aisle, her little elbows swinging beside her body, blond curls bouncing, eyes shining, and with a big smile on her face. The two of them squeezed past me and settled into their seats. "Mommy, Mommy!" Janel began, "I saw him. He's there!"

"Who?" I asked, thinking she meant the pilot or copilot. But she said, "Santa! We saw Santa!"

"Who?" I had no idea what had happened in the cockpit.

Their words tangled in a muddle as they tried to explain that Santa was flying up in the air, a little bit ahead of our plane. They had seen him with their own eyes on this round, green radar screen. There was a big blop with lots of little blops ahead of it. *That* was Santa and *those* were the reindeer. Santa was flying just ahead of us. "He knows! He knows where we're going," Janel beamed. "He's already going to be there when we get there." The joy we felt was beyond containment. It spilled all over my soul.

I fought back tears. However in the world could that pilot have known that my little blond Japanese-born American daughter was brokenhearted, not knowing exactly where she was going and afraid that no matter where, Santa wouldn't find her by morning. God had arranged it. God was way ahead of the flight attendant, ahead of the pilot, ahead of the plane, and ahead of us. He took awesome care of us at 36,000 feet and would take care of us our whole lives. God cared about two little girls' Christmas. And a widow's.

We were exhausted by the time we finally stood in my parents' home in Manila late that Christmas Eve but not too tired to notice a rather anemic, spindly palm Dad had turned into a Christmas tree by attaching to it an odd assortment of ornaments. Mom wasn't feeling well so he had tackled the job of making the tree glittery and sparkly for the girls. I couldn't help but notice there were no presents beneath it. I had a few small gifts in my suitcase, and I went to bed preparing myself for a sparse Christmas. The important thing, I insisted as I drifted off to sleep, was that we were together as family.

On Christmas morning, Barra and Janel woke me early and pulled me down the stairs to the tree. All three of us stopped and stared. Obviously, Santa knew *exactly* where we were! Heaps of presents, in every size and shape, wrapped in shiny papers and tied with satin bows, sparkled before us. The little palm looked like it was floating in an ocean of color. Later I learned that word had gone out that I was taking the girls to my parents. Friends and supporters from the States and Manila sent packages for my daughters, which my parents hid until Christmas morning. Weeks earlier God started this wonderful morning with a letter promising to pay for airfares, then gave us a Christmas we would never, ever forget.

The years quickly slipped by. I was busy with family, radio work, supervising staff, day-to-day responsibilities, and giving on-air broadcasts of adult programs. When the girls were just seven and nine, they had their own broadcast for young children that they did in the Japanese language. Amazing, really, that my father could be heard broadcasting via short wave from Manila, I could be heard in English from Tokyo, and my children could also be heard broadcasting in Japanese. It was quite unusual for three generations to be regularly on the air waves, and the girls not even speaking in their birth language!

The ministry of FEBC grew and expanded and reached the point when western leadership was turned over to national leadership. The transition was the right thing, the needed thing, the planned thing, but still so traumatic. I found it hard to let go of the ministry David and I poured our lives into. Twenty-one years of my life belonged to Japan and I found it almost impossible to imagine life any other way.

We packed our belongings and prepared for the day we would board a plane and fly to another foreign country. Japan-born Janel was fourteen and Okinawa-born Barra was sixteen when we arrived in California. We felt like aliens after having been away from the United States for so long. I accepted a new assignment in the home office of FEBC, the girls attended school, and the new environment was a never-ending daily culture shock.

In Japan higher education is revered, and David felt to have real impact there, he needed to obtain his Master's degree. He completed the requirements during one of our furloughs. I, too, enrolled in a Master's program at a university in Tokyo, but after David's death, with heavy and new responsibilities as Directrix of FEBC, I had to drop out of my graduate program. There simply wasn't time to pursue my degree. But the girls had caught our love of learning and within a few years, each had graduated from Biola University. When Janel was just 23, she tucked her Master's degree in her packet of achievements.

Then in 1997, Barra and her husband, Janel's husband and I applauded loud and long as we watched 31-year-old Janel receive a Ph.D. in Intercultural Education. I thought back to her very first day of school in Japan and remembered how a swat on the bottom from a loving father figure sent her courageously on her way. And now that little girl, long blond hair still bobbing in ringlets, was receiving a well-earned doctorate.

I cried, clapped, and cheered like any proud mother. Then, just minutes later, Janel and Barra got their turn to cry and clap for me. The president of Biola shared some of my life story with thousands gathered for the graduation ceremonies. When I was called to the platform, it was as if God said, "You were willing to give up your Master's to do what you needed to do for my sake. Now it's your turn." After my story was told, I too was hooded by the university. The crowd responded with a thunderous ovation as I bowed to an L.L.D., an honorary Doctor of Laws. Barra, Janel, and I knew in our hearts only God could have brought us to this place.

I was a preacher's daughter, missionary kid, university graduate, wife, missionary, mother, and widow by age 36. But my best title was still ahead. After the graduation festivities, my two little grandsons presented me with a wooden name plate for my desk: Doctor Grandma George. Without any doubt, that's the best. But each title is extraordinary to me, because through them God showed his faithfulness.

When my girls saw Santa on a radar screen, I knew that God was going before us, not just to Manila, but in every step of our every day. When I saw a heap of gifts beneath a simply decorated little palm, I knew he would never leave us without the support of much love. In the silence of one Christmas Eve, I cried myself to sleep, fearing a morning of disappointment. But I woke to find, once again, that God is the Giver of all good gifts. No matter where we are.

fifteen

"Peace on Earth"
More than a Phrase

Máire ("MOY-a") is the epitome of all things Irish. She is the voice of Clannad ("family"), an aptly named band that, over a 28-year span, has included her brothers, sisters, and twin uncles. Their Celtic albums have sold over 15 million copies worldwide and their instantly recognizable music is featured in movie soundtracks, British TV series, and international commercials. A musical force in Europe, Máire's acclaimed duet with U2 lead singer Bono and her first solo album, *Perfect Time,* launched her popularity in the United States.

The oldest of nine children, Máire grew up in a Gaelic-speaking home where she and her siblings sang to the accompaniment of her mother's piano and her father's accordion. Her music contains the sounds of Irish instruments, the lyric of two languages, and two truths. Since childhood she has observed in her beloved country, once called the Land of Saints and Scholars, the sad conflict among neighbors, families, and counties. In a land of great religious tradition and exquisite ancient prayers, her divided country finds little peace among those who celebrate the birth of the Prince of Peace. Those who dance to the music of heaven pray that someday right will prevail and the Irish will sing the hymn of "peace on earth, good will to men."

Máire's Story

I was seven years old when I first held a ballet comic book in my hands. On those thin, vibrantly colored pages were graceful ballerinas; lithe and lanky, lovely and elegant. I had done Irish dancing since I could walk, arms held rigid against my stiff body, loose legs kicking and tapping. But this dancing looked different and so beautiful. I began to dream of being a ballerina.

I grew up in Gweedore, a little town perched on the rugged northwest tip of Ireland. I loved the wide-open spaces, rolling mountains, and craggy cliffs. I didn't have many toys and hardly ever saw the sweets and goodies pictured in magazines, but my life was full to overflowing with imagination and energy. What I didn't have, I didn't miss! Most of all, I had my many brothers and sisters to play with. In our garden, we had a pretend shop full of all the old cans and boxes that we could find. We made a seesaw from an old plank and barrel. We played in the river and fished for trout and salmon teeming in from the cold Atlantic. We joined windswept old fellas on the peat bogs as they slurped strong, sweet tea between bursts of turf cutting. We ran for miles along the endless white beaches that fringed the jagged coastline.

In the back of my mind, no matter what game we played, I was a ballerina. I could hardly wait for each week's edition of the ballet comic so I could copy the new steps. Soon I realized that this was not enough and pestered my mammy and daddy to take me to proper ballet classes. I might as well have been asking them to fly me to the moon. We lived in County Donegal, and the nearest ballet teacher was in Derry, a two-and-a-half hour drive from Gweedore along twisting, narrow roads. Besides, the lessons were too expensive, and my parents contented themselves by thinking this whim of mine would pass. My girlish heart, however, thought differently. Taking ballet lessons was my dream and I wasn't going to let go without a struggle.

Eventually my parents gave in, maybe because they tired of my constant twirling and spinning around the house. I don't know how they found the name of Mrs. Watson or how they arranged for me to join her class, but I leapt with joy when they told me they had arranged for my first lesson.

That Saturday morning, and for many more to follow, I tumbled out of bed and with breakfast still in my mouth jumped into my Dad's old Austin for the long drive over the mountains and around Loch Swilly, until the grey, busy buildings of Derry appeared around the swirling Foyle. This weekly pilgrimage drew me closer to my fantasy world of tiptoes and tripping, of daintiness and delicacy, of the melodies of Mozart and Tchaikovsky. The drive became the lifeline to my childhood fantasies. The long trip that first day was not so much a journey with a destination, but more an excursion into my dreamworld. I had a dream in my heart but I didn't know exactly what to expect as we drove past Mount Errigal, the highest mountain in Donegal, and Dunlewy Lake and the Poison Glen with its misty history, then past the Haunted House and the Hungry House, two solid stone cottages alone on the rolling hills.

To pass the time during our trip, my daddy, an enthusiastic storyteller, told tales and scary legends about the landmarks. I had heard these stories hundreds of times, but I never tired of hearing them again. When we passed the majestic Glenveagh Castle, we craned our necks to catch a glimpse of the green manicured gardens sweeping down to its own lake. My daddy told of the English squire, John George Adair, who evicted his Irish tenants from the beautiful land in 1870 to build the castle, and of the last owner, Henry P. McIlhenny, who made his fortune from little bottles of Tabasco and who took residence by throwing extravagant parties and banquets. My daddy played in showbands when he was younger and often performed in the castle, entertaining the socialites and celebrities gathered in this isolated place. His stories conjured up images of a world far from my own.

I was trembling with excitement when we drove into Derry and eventually located Mrs. Watson's big corner house at the top of Clarendon Street. The housekeeper greeted us at the front door and led us up a long staircase to the first floor. I heard piano music as we approached a closed door, and my heart pounded with trepidation. The door let us into what must have been the biggest room I had ever seen in a home. The side wall was completely covered in mirrors, with a long, wooden bar running along the middle. Mirrors on the back of the room reflected light from two large windows on the opposite end. A shiny black piano, adorned with a single beautiful old lamp, majestically commanded one corner. A woman named Mrs. Wallace sat on the stool playing dance pieces that would soon become familiar to me. A group of girls sat in chairs and on a bench, changing into their dancing shoes.

If I had been feeling a touch bashful when I entered the room, this now suddenly changed to overwhelming embarrassment. I didn't own any ballet shoes. Derry was the only place I could buy a pair, but I didn't want to be late on my first day, so we had gone straight to my lesson. Mrs. Watson took my hand, fully aware I had no shoes, and announced that it was entirely proper to dance barefoot on the first day. She then turned to my parents and told them to come back for me at 12:30.

Help! I did not know this was going to happen and I immediately felt very alone. The room was full of all kinds of girls, so different from the four school girls my age in Gweedore. These girls were immaculately dressed, their beautiful hair neatly groomed and tied at the back. They spoke English with lovely soft accents. Gaelic was my first language and I had learned English at school, but I felt quite unsure of it in this place. The wooden floor shook beneath me. Would I come across as a stupid country girl? I desperately wanted to learn ballet, but at that moment I felt very naive amongst these cultured budding ballerinas.

With a double clap to get our attention, Mrs. Watson called us into a circle. A girl reached out and took my hand, then guided me in what to do. She whispered, "My name is Alison." I looked around nervously as we started to dance, expecting to stand out clumsily like a sore thumb, but after a few minutes, I got the hang of the simple steps and began to enjoy myself. My shy expression relaxed into a broad smile as I realized that here I was, at last, dancing ballet. Before I knew it, the class was over! What a thrill it had been. Everyone was so friendly and caring towards each other and to me. It didn't seem to matter that I was a country girl. Alison waved goodbye with a smile and that was the beginning of our friendship.

My parents picked me up, took me to buy ballet shoes, and treated me to lunch. It was probably the most wonderful day of my life.

Considering the fact I lived so far away, Mrs. Watson arranged for me to come to group lessons every other Saturday and then stay for an extra, private lesson. My love for ballet knew no bounds. Every afternoon, I furiously practiced newly learned steps, prancing around the sitting room, dancing to any music that came on the radio, much to the annoyance of an ever-increasing brood of brothers and sisters. But, since I was the eldest, their protests fell on deaf ears.

Because I had four brothers and four sisters, it was increasingly difficult for my mother to drive to Derry and sit around for a couple of hours. So it became my father's lot to drive me, then sit in the car and read the paper from cover to cover on ballet Saturdays. Only now can I appreciate what sacrifices my parents made to make my dream come true. But they both knew about dreams. My father spent most of his life on the road with his showband, but as he now had a large family to feed, he had recently bought a pub so he could stay at home and still sing and play his accordion every night. My mother's love of music was expressed by teaching it in the local school. Still, despite both livelihoods, there were many mouths to feed and from a financial point of view, my ballet classes must have made a big dent in the family's budget.

When I got older, I was able to take the bus to Derry on ballet Saturdays. It stopped near my house at a quarter to eight and dropped me close to Clarendon Street around 11:30, just in time for the lesson. Manus, the bus conductor, was our neighbor and he virtually guaranteed my safety to Mammy and Daddy. He was a kind man with a big smile who told stories and jokes as the old bus bumped along the mountain roads. When my younger sister, Deirdre, was old enough, she began taking ballet with me. It was a huge responsibility for me to look after her, but we always enjoyed the ride and shared the excitement of our dance class.

My sister and I made a lot of friends among the other girls. We all had one thing in common, and it had nothing to do with where we came from, how we spoke, or what we were called. As children, we had no idea how soon our innocence would be shattered. Even if we had seen it coming, we still would not have believed how our lives would change or how our friendships would be irreparably damaged by circumstances beyond our control.

By now, we moved easily between one another's homes for lunch after class. It didn't matter what part of Derry we went to, whether it was a large or small house, whether it was tidy or untidy. What mattered was that we were friends. The fact that our ballet class was made up of girls from both Protestant and Catholic backgrounds made no difference to us in those early days.

There was something brewing, though. I overheard snippets of grown-up conversations about civil rights and marches. But as a country child from Gweedore, I was fairly unaware of the growing tension in Northern Ireland. I didn't know about slums and discrimination. I didn't understand the fury of the Catholics who, even with the best qualifications in the world, were unable to get jobs simply because of how and where they worshiped God. Nor did I comprehend that a political system based on the premise of "one house, one vote" was loaded in favor of the Protestant land and business owners. Many of the poor Catholic families had as many as three generations living under one roof, yet only the head of the house could vote in the elections. Financial, political, and social power was concentrated in the Protestant community and discontentment in the province was about to spill out onto the streets. I didn't have to understand the reasons to notice that something was happening.

In the autumn of 1967, my ballet class excitedly prepared for our Christmas show. It would be a big production—the highlight of our year—a chance to show off newfound skills to our parents and to the general public. Because we often paired off to practice our steps and dances, Alison and I naturally gravitated toward each other. A bond had developed between us in the four years since that first day when she made me feel so welcome. I had often been to her house and loved her family and her cheerful, happy-go-lucky parents.

One Saturday, Alison and I were tying the ribbons on our ballet shoes, waiting for the class to begin when a couple of local girls came in, talking at the top of their voices. Heaven knows what they had been talking about, but the words, "I'm so glad I'm not a Protestant" rang through the air as if a gun had been fired in our midst. Everyone in the room froze. Slowly I turned to look at Alison seated beside me. Our eyes met for a fraction of a second then she swiftly turned away, embarrassed and devastated. Our cozy world was shattered by a few words.

I suppose at some stage even children had to be affected by the hatred that was splitting our country and now here it was. Alison was Protestant and I was Catholic. Protestants did ballet, Catholics did Irish dancing! In the weeks that passed after that bombshell, we struggled to ignore its effect. Alison and I continued to dance and practice together, each putting on a brave face. All the other girls tried to attempt an air of civility and friendship, but it was hopeless. Factions developed in the changing rooms. Whispering and sniggering replaced our familiar camaraderie. We all arrived, did our lesson, and then left. The joy and the thrill of dance were fading. Only the shared goal of perfecting our Christmas program motivated us.

Mrs. Watson, to her credit, managed to hold things together and kept our focus on the Christmas show. Whether it was the true spirit of Christmas or just an obstinate determination not to let the cruel world into the showpiece, we rehearsed our dances and moves with a passion long forgotten. There was still talk of marches for civil rights, of accusations and repercussions on the outside, but inside our first-floor room on Clarendon Street, we closed our eyes and ears and prepared for the gala performance at the Guild-hall. I had a feeling it would be the last performance for me.

All of us ballerinas were determined to do something together. After all, whatever else drove us apart, we knew, at the back of our minds, that celebrating the birth of Jesus was important for all of us and carried the same message whether Protestant or Catholic. In our introduction into the adult world of war, we prepared to herald the birth of the Prince of Peace.

The big night arrived. I had come to Derry with Deirdre and other members of my family earlier in the day. During our final dress rehearsal, Mammy and Daddy finished their last bit of Christmas shopping. With the escalating turmoil in Northern Ireland, my parents had decided that our trips to ballet classes would end after Christmas. This, then, was my swan song, an abrupt end to a period of my life which had made my heart sing and my feet move as never before. Alison and I never spoke of the wedge driven between us. As we changed into our costumes and prepared for the evening show, we felt the nervous excitement customary before such performances. But not a word was spoken of what would happen afterwards, of Christmas, or the coming year.

We knew this was the end. For one night, we pretended that the trouble was not about to start, that there was no fence separating us, and that the joy and wonder of Christmas was for all of us to share in exactly the same way.

We stood in the wings of the Guildhall stage and peeked around the curtains searching for our families in the audience. The music started up with Mrs. Wallace on the grand piano and a small orchestra in front of the stage. The colored lights came up and we were on. Mrs. Watson had obviously taught us well. For the next two hours our only thoughts were about our steps, formations, and timing. We danced perfectly—a team of little individuals wanting our parents to be proud of us, but more than that, wanting to please each other.

Afterwards the changing room was abuzz with girlish laughter and purest joy. Never before had we experienced such excitement or such an exhilarating rush of energy and adrenaline. We were all over Mrs. Watson, who could hardly contain the tears of happiness and pride she felt for us.

Then it was time to say goodbye to Mrs. Watson and to the others. And to Alison. Our bags were packed and our parents were waiting for us in the corridor outside. I started to say something to Alison but the words dried up. We grasped each other's hands for one last time, and squeezed our fingers together in a final, desperate outpouring of silent emotion. We embraced each other in a big hug. I don't remember who let go first, but we turned away from each other and I walked to the door. I turned for one last look at my dear friends. Waves and smiles flew at me from all directions but one. At the far end of the room stood Alison with her back to me, rigid, and for her own reasons refusing to turn around. I took a deep breath and walked into the winter night holding my daddy's hand.

Not a word was said in the car on the long drive home.

I HEARD THE BELLS ON CHRISTMAS DAY

I heard the bells on Christmas day
Their old familiar carols play
And wild and sweet the words repeat
Of peace on earth, good will to men.

I thought how, as the day had come,
The belfries of all Christendom
had rolled along th' unbroken song
Of peace on earth, good will to men.

And in despair I bowed my head:
"There is no peace on earth," I said,
"For hate is strong, and mocks the song
Of peace on earth, good will to men."

Then pealed the bells more loud and deep:
"God is not dead, nor doth He sleep;
The wrong shall fail, the right prevail,
With peace on earth, good will to men."

Till ringing, singing on its way,
The world revolved from night to day—
A voice, a chime, a chant sublime
Of peace on earth, good will to men.

    —Henry W. Longfellow

sixteen

Giving Love Away

Shirley Caesar has a room full of bronze, silver, glass, and gold statues, each one representing either a Grammy, Stellar, Dove, Soul Train, or another of her numerous awards. She has been honored by the NAACP and *Essence* magazine for her achievements in the arts. Recipient of two honorary doctorates, Shirley is currently enrolled in the Master of Divinity program at Duke University. Still, the awards and trophies she has received do not characterize her as well as what she gives away. Giving to others is what is most important to Shirley.

The child singer once called "Baby Shirley" by audiences across the United States is now called Pastor Shirley by the congregation of the Mt. Calvary Word of Faith Church in Raleigh, North Carolina. The world knows her as the energetic and electrifying "First Lady of Gospel Music." She refers to herself as "a down-to-earth singer serving an up-to-date God, a traditional gospel singer with a contemporary flavor, a woman young in spirit who loves the Lord." She is indeed all of those things, but the poor and needy in Durham and Raleigh know her as a generous benefactor, especially during the Christmas season.

Shirley's Story

Let me tell you, I find that Christmas is often the saddest time for poor people. There are times when my husband and I buy clothes and take them into one of the most deprived communities around here. We tuck a $50 bill or some amount of money underneath the new clothes for the children. Then we knock on some family's door and when they answer, we say, "This is something we just wanted to give to you and your children. Merry Christmas."

I inherited this openhanded generosity in my childhood and try to base my life on the way we used to spend Christmas when I was a little girl: giving and sharing. I *love* Christmas! Love it, love it! In December, you can hear a different sound in my voice, because that's the happiest time of the whole year for me. I mean the happiest time! As a child, I loved to trim my mama's tree with ornaments and lights to make it festive. Because she was a semi-invalid, I'd open her bedroom door so she could enjoy the Christmas holidays from the chair in her room.

Our whole Christmas was built around Mama. Before any of the twelve of us, five boys and seven girls, were allowed to open gifts on Christmas morning, we all went in the living room and gathered around the tree. Mama sat in her own chair and led us in a Christmas carol and a prayer. Then everybody, each one of us, had to give a testimony. We'd thank God for bringing us to another Christmas. We'd thank him that our circle had not been broken. We were thankful for Mama. It was a tradition 40 years ago and it's still a tradition.

Even as adults, we gathered around Mama each Christmas, up to five generations of us together at her house, until she passed. Now only seven of her children are alive, but we get together on Christmas Day at my house with our spouses, children, grandchildren, and great-grandchildren. As more and more little children are born into the family, we teach them to be thankful when they learn to talk. We say, "I thank God," then let the baby echo us. Then we add, "for mama," and the baby repeats after us again. This way we've passed the tradition from generation to generation.

Because we're scattered around the country, not everyone can be here every year. Still, at least 100 are here to celebrate. Do we ever! Add to all of the relatives who come for Christmas our friends from out-of-town, church members, and the people they invite and sometimes as many as 200 people crowd into my house for the day. I think they like the way I celebrate Christmas on a large scale! One or two cooks are hired to prepare all the food in time for our dinner. I hear people say things like, "Honey, you haven't enjoyed a Christmas until you go to Shirley Caesar's house!"

After we give our testimonies of thanks to the Lord, we sing some more Christmas carols, but by this time, the children want to jump under that tree and open the pile of gifts!

At one time, the family started drawing names, but before I knew it, somebody would buy me a gift and then somebody else would buy another person a gift. So we stopped pulling names and started buying presents for everybody. With so many relatives, that's a lot of gifts! It didn't matter if we spent one dollar or ten, we love giving to each other.

Each person who comes in our house receives a Christmas gift. I start shopping for Christmas in August and hide all the gifts in the house. In fact, I hide them so well, I sometimes find them after Christmas! I buy a lot of neckties and different sized shirts and dresses in various colors and sizes. Well, what can I say? The Lord has given me a spirit of giving and sharing. I even recorded a Christmas song, "Giving and Sharing." So everyone receives something. EVERYBODY!

Let me tell you about this past Christmas. We decorated the house with lights every place I could put them. I just love lights inside the house. Cooks were preparing Christmas dinner, friends and church members and family were wrapping gifts, and the lights were on all over the house. Bells chimed out Christmas music and loud banging and delicious aromas came out of the kitchen. It was a noisy, wonderful, exciting time.

But then, early on Christmas morning, after being up most of the night, I thought about all of the people coming—nearly 200! I said, "Lord, I can't bring all of these people in my house." I remembered the previous year when antiques were broken and one of the doors was knocked down by exuberant kids racing up and down the stairs all day long. I knew I couldn't do it like that anymore. I wanted to celebrate Christmas with everyone and still protect my house, so I decided to move our celebration to a larger place.

I got on the phone and called all the local hotels until I finally found an open ballroom. Then I called family members and told them that our Christmas location had been changed. Two hundred people still showed up! People and food filled the room. The hotel provided a big screen TV, but no tree.

Because we made the arrangements so late, I didn't get a chance to put up a Christmas tree. But with all the visiting and laughing and gift exchanging and eating, I don't think too many people missed it. With 200 people, there wasn't time for everyone to give their testimony, but we all felt the spirit of giving and sharing. I've already decided that we're going to do it this way again next year. If the ballroom isn't already decorated, we'll go in there before Christmas Eve and do it up like I decorate my house. We'll even do the all-night wrapping party there.

Leaving the house led to a new opportunity to give. On our way into the hotel early that day, we met a young girl standing in front of the hotel doors. It was obvious she was living on the streets. I invited her to join us, then privately paid for a room for her to sleep in for a few nights, gave her some cash for food, and as she still had no place to go, arranged an offering at my church to give her a new start. I've learned that the more I give, the more God gives back to me! I don't have a whole lot, but I take what I have and give it back to the Lord, and the Lord keeps giving to me. It's like a circle: God puts it in my right hand, I move it to my left hand and give it away, and God fills my right hand again. That's how God works. He keeps right on blessing you because you keep on blessing somebody.

My circle of giving and sharing neither starts nor stops with my family, friends, or the occasional stranger. My Christmas giving begins each year with the Christmas Give-Away sponsored by the Shirley Caesar Outreach Ministry, Inc., a non-profit organization I founded nearly thirty years ago. Fifty percent of whatever I earn on the road is given back to the Lord by blessing needy families. I buy thousands and thousands of pounds of chicken and canned goods and hundreds of loaves of bread, including helpful items like T-shirts, soap, potatoes, and yams. It's a good thing I'm a seasoned shopper!

The Shirley Caesar Christmas Give-Away is held at a church in Durham. We load up bags with all the food and goods and distribute them to the poor. If anything's left over, I bring it to my church in Raleigh later the same day for the needy people in our own neighborhoods. When I first started, I asked people to donate tricycles or bikes their children had outgrown. Years ago, kids didn't care whether toys were used or brand-new, as long as they got something. Today's children are a little bit more particular so we've found companies to donate new toys for us to give away:

dolls, stuffed animals, games, and action figures from movies to the latest cartoon characters.

My church has also adopted the giving tradition. During the holidays, we put out a big barrel and people drop wrapped gifts into it and they hang clean, used clothes on rows of racks. Then the local radio stations and community newspapers announce the day and time for the annual Give-Away. The spirit of giving has broken out like wildfire in the Raleigh-Durham area. In fact, here I am known as much for my giving as I am for my singing— almost more so.

I wish they hadn't, but when we first started this program, people tried to take advantage of the Give-Away by getting in line several times. We learned how to be better organized to limit that behavior. Now, we take names a week earlier and then call them out in alphabetical order during the Give-Away. Some say, "I came to pick up for so-and-so." I don't know if they're telling the truth, but I can't say no. If someone says, "Pastor Caesar, I didn't get a chance to get my name on the list. Could I have a bag anyway?" we make sure they leave with something.

If there's a family with five or more children, we'll give them two or three bags to make sure they have enough for more than one meal. We try to be generous and fill the bags to overflowing with bread, ham, chicken, and canned goods. We're giving back to the Lord for his birthday. Since we can't give directly to Jesus, we give to those he told us to help. He gave himself to us, so we give ourselves back to the people. I'm convinced that serving God is serving people. When I look around and see the smiles on the faces of children of all races and nationalities, I realize it's worth all the work, effort, and money.

The Give-Away is about more than giving *things,* however. It is about giving people a chance to start a new life with Christ. Some of the poor we serve are drug addicts and alcoholics. Some of the young women have been so misused and abused that they look years older than they are. Before the Give-Away, we have a program in the sanctuary that gives me a chance to talk about

Jesus and invite them to church. We sing Christmas carols to really get us all in the spirit of the season. I tell them, "I can only give you one meal, but better than that, I can show you how to continue your life. If I can go back to school, so can you." I'll call one up to the stage, maybe one whose life has really been battered from drug abuse, and let her know underneath all of her pain is a beautiful girl. I tell her she is loved and give her a big hug. This is ministry for me. I'm good at throwing my arms around someone, hugging them and embracing them and letting them know they don't have to allow the enemy to steal their life and their youth.

People in the audience who've come to get food will sometimes testify of their thanks to God for keeping them alive to see another Christmas. Some have testimonies of healing. One said simply, "Please pray for me. My life is messed up from drugs, and I'm tired of it. I want to be free." I know for a fact that a lot of them don't want to keep going back to drugs, but they're just so addicted. I let them know that God gave them gifts and ministries, and that he wants to use them while they're young and strong.

Right after the Give-Away, my husband and I go straight to the hospital. I visit room to room and pray for the sick and wish them a Merry Christmas. I know it's kind of sad for them being there, but I just remind them that it's Jesus' birthday and tell them, "You may be here, but your heart can be glad that God has given us his wonderful Son." Sometimes I'll sing a song.

I also visit those in jail. Pizza, soda, and cake are provided by the jail and I provide the music. I may never have any of the prisoners as a church member, but I don't even care about that. I just want them to know that somebody in the community cares. Sometimes at the jail, I see kids, young people, and even older folks I used to know. When they see me, some try to hide their faces but others are as glad to see me as I am to see them. We throw our arms around each other in a big hug.

That's what I love about Christmas—giving to people because I love them. I believe the main prerequisite of being a pastor is loving people. In honesty, I must admit there have been times when I have felt used. People sometimes try to take advantage of my generosity, but I don't mind. People ran to Jesus, wanting a miracle or a meal, and then after they were healed or fed, they walked away from him. I'm trying to follow his example and give as freely as he gave. I love everybody. I don't see color. I don't see gender. I don't care where they are in their personal lives—alcoholics, drug users, poor, rich, relatives, or strangers. I throw my arms around them because I love them the way I love Christmas.

I enjoy my Give-Away as much as I enjoy Christmas morning. It's really just more of what my mama taught me. I give the Lord his gift first by giving to others. That's the way my husband and I do it. Before we give our own family or friends a gift, we make sure the Lord has his gift first by giving to the needy.

Christmas and a Carpenter's Saw

Crystal Lewis appears fearless as she belts out song after song before the thousands gathered at Franklin Graham Crusades and Harvest Crusades with Greg Laurie. Her faith and artistry take her from the stages of the Crusades and the Grammy Awards to church platforms in North America and outdoor arenas in South America. "Incomparable" is the word most often used to describe Crystal. She sings and performs like no other.

Wife and mother, songwriter and arranger, performer and business woman, it seems there is little that she hasn't accomplished. There are few awards or accolades this sensitive singer has not already received.

Yet a recent Christmas morning turned her attention from success as an artist to the fearful potential of missing the meaning of Christmas. She learned that strength is sometimes found in frailty, and that taking risks for the sake of right is something not to be feared.

CRYSTAL'S STORY

A brunette, a blond, and a redhead, born in four-year intervals, my sisters and I were the three Cs: Cryssie, Candi, and Cassie. Ah, how sweet! From the moment we were born, our mom, Mary, taught us to love music. We all remember toddling around the piano, listening to her play. We loved the sound of her flawlessly rich voice that covered every range—alto, soprano, tenor—well, maybe not bass! Mom's gifts as an accomplished pianist and clarinetist, song arranger and composer, laid the foundation for our own musical achievements.

My sister Candace, the middle child, sings beautifully and plays the piano and French horn. When she was about eighteen she taught herself electric bass and knocked us off our feet by becoming such a funky player! Jazz, rock, she plays it all! Not only is she a great musician, she's completing her Ph.D. in medical physics right now at UCLA. She's extremely well rounded, this girl. And if that's not enough, just eight months ago she had her first baby!

My youngest sister, Cassandra, follows the family's musical tradition by playing the piano and singing. We call her Sister Teresa (she's not old enough to be called Mother Teresa) because her life is committed to inner-city missions. She's incredibly compassionate, unbelievably so, the very personification of self-sacrifice. She'd be mad at me for describing her as a literal angel, but she really is a unique individual.

I played piano through college but my voice was my main instrument. When I was seventeen I recorded my first album and a few years later joined the cast of Nickelodeon's "Roundhouse." Out of all the projects I've done, including six in Spanish, one of my favorites is the recent Christmas album I recorded with my mom and sisters. It was so nostalgic—we three girls being told what to sing by Mom!

Since Dad was the pastor of our church, we sang with our mom as a quartet a lot on Sunday mornings, Sunday nights, Wednesday nights, and during revivals...it's a Nazarene thing! A tradition, really, of family, church, and music.

Dad's the one who started another important tradition in our family. Every Christmas Eve day he drove the whole family to an inner-city mission in Los Angeles where he preached, my sisters and I sang with Mom, and Dorothy Flannigan played her saw. No joke, a saw. The metal thing that cuts wood.

Dorothy, a member of our church, took a great big saw, placed the handle between her knees and held the metal end in her left hand. She moved a big old violin or cello bow across the teeth of that thing and made that sucker SING! She got great vibrato and tone when she played "Amazing Grace." It was a sight! And a sound! As a kid, of course, I found it hysterical to watch. But...did she ever make music.

For years, every Christmas Eve day, we did exactly the same thing: Dad preached, we sang, Dorothy played, and afterwards those who endured the entire program got a turkey and dressing dinner, a shower, and a bed for the night.

One year, probably when I was ten years old, we made our annual Christmas Eve pilgrimage to the mission. The crowd at the front of the door was so tight we couldn't get in. So, without a hint of hesitation, Dad led us down the alley to enter through a back door. I remember thinking, *I cannot believe my parents are letting me do this—it's dangerous—and weird!* We actually stepped over a body sleeping in the street. My parents acted as though that was nothing unusual. I remember being afraid of the smell of poverty and the sight of destitution, but I don't recall any fear in my parents, ever. I watched them in the ministry, going in to hospitals and funeral homes to meet crying and grieving families. I watched them serve and help all kinds of people, so I know my fear didn't come from them. It obviously came from the enemy, who always tries to thwart the work of God in our lives. Regardless, I was not comfortable in situations both my parents and my sisters moved in easily.

As the years went by, I felt that being on the stage exempted me from doing the hard, rolling-up-the-sleeves kind of dirty work. Even now I'm inclined to rationalize, "I can't do that because of who I am and what I do. My gift is singing. Serving food to the homeless is someone else's spiritual gift."

I'm not sure if that's an excuse. I know we're all called to serve in different capacities, using our own talents and gifts. Keith Green wrote lyrics that said something like, "Oh that's not my calling" or "That's not my gift." He was being sarcastic, but when I first heard the song, the words pierced me and made me admit that I used that very argument as an excuse all the time. I used that reasoning to avoid doing work that made me uncomfortable. Ironically, my youngest sister, Cassie, virtually lives right in the middle of the downtrodden, the hurting, and the poor. That's her spiritual gift, and she's not at all afraid. The example of her ministry and her fearlessness has helped me look at other people, and myself, differently.

Lately, I've been facing some issues of fear, and I admit one of those is the fear of serving in the inner city. And I've learned that fear isn't only felt in strange situations or in uncomfortable circumstances. For instance, this past Christmas Day definitely frightened me. I watched in horror as my children and their six cousins ripped open Christmas gifts at their Gramma's house. Eight children, all under age seven, shredded paper from boxes, barely looked at the gift, yelped if they were happy or cried if it wasn't exactly right, then tossed it aside, yelling, "Where's my next one?" The potential of my own children's selfishness scared me. I watched them get caught up in a clamor we adults actually arranged for them and thought, "This is not Christmas. I don't want them to think this is what Christmas is all about. I don't want this for my kids or my nieces or nephews. They need to know the real meaning of Christmas." On the way home that night, I asked my son and daughter what they received and who gave them which gifts. They didn't know and I was appalled.

Even though I was a little afraid to do it, I wrote a letter to the family suggesting that next year we let the cousins draw names and exchange gifts, like the adults. Each grandchild would get two gifts: one from a cousin and one from their grandparents. I admitted that my kids were learning all too well the attitude of "Give me more." I suggested that as an alternative we could take the eight cousins to sing carols at a retirement home or attend a church service together. Being an in-law, I didn't want to overstep my position, but, fortunately, everyone else agreed.

As I wrote out my thoughts, my mind jumped back to one Christmas Eve day when I was about fourteen or fifteen. The Los Angeles mission my family went to was now feeding thousands of people. The building was too small to hold everyone, so the mission blocked off the street, erected a chain link fence for crowd control, and set out rows of long tables on the asphalt. Groups from several churches were scheduled to preach and sing in a continuous program throughout the day, serving the poor and homeless who waited their turn in a line that wound down the sidewalk and around several blocks.

The procession of preachers and singers came and went on schedule. Everything went as planned—except for one thing. It rained. It rained and rained. Which was frightening considering we were standing under a makeshift canopy hurriedly thrown up over a wobbly portable stage. The mission had provided a little electric keyboard that my mother just hated playing because it didn't have full octaves like a real piano. We sang into a cheap Karaoke-type microphone that was hooked up to an inefficient boom box. I was young and have to admit a little put out by the less than acceptable quality of equipment. After all, I had already been in the studio a couple of times and felt this whole thing was a little beneath me. My attitude bordered on, "I'm too good for this" and "Is it time to go yet?"

I stood on that rickety stage, afraid of being electrocuted, and peered out from beneath the covering of the flimsy canopy. I vividly remember looking through the chain link fence at a woman pushing three small children in a shopping cart. I watched those children watch us sing, and wondered, "What are they thinking?" They were dirty, wet, and probably hungry, crammed into a metal basket, listening to my sisters and me sing.

Their big eyes stared out of filthy faces and I stared back, asking myself, "Why am I here and they there?" What unfair chain of events led that mother and her three children to stand on one side of the fence, while my mother and her three well-dressed children stood on this side? Strange new feelings of compassion ached in my heart.

I turned back toward the tables and saw hundreds of volunteers serving the homeless. A few were movie stars, some were TV celebrities, hoping to be noticed by the reporters and news cameras. But most of the volunteers just wanted to serve, wanted to do something kind for people who weren't often treated well. As the rain continued to fall, some of the volunteers surrounded the tables and lifted their arms over their heads, stretching big blue tarps over the seated people. They got drenched as they stood in the rain, tethered to plastic sheets in their effort to keep the poor dry. I watched teenagers and seniors, adults beside young children, provide shelter for people whose usual shelter was cardboard boxes, street grates, or bus stops.

I had been in my dad's church all my life, and had seen wonderful people do wonderful things for each other. But I had never seen anything like this. Tarps suspended by human flagpoles in a downpour of rain. My mind yelled, "This is Jesus! This is what the Bible is talking about!"

My eyes saw a vision, in a sense, of the real meaning of giving, the real essence of Christmas. I had been raised with a lot of gifts and with a lot of great friends in my life, but here I saw a band of volunteers give the gift of love and a hot meal to strangers. I know how easy it is to be critical of those less fortunate. Some think they're undeserving, unable to totally appreciate or even understand what was being given to them. Or that it's their own fault that they're dirty, out of work, maybe even drugged or drunk. Yet none of that mattered. The volunteers gave the gift anyway, because that's what they were called to do. As Christians, we're all supposed to give selflessly, leaving judgment to God.

That year I was a typical teenager with a bad attitude. I knew a lot more than my parents did, or so I thought at the time. But when I saw that mother with her kids in a shopping cart, for the first time in my life, I felt real, heart-breaking compassion.

Years later, when writing the letter to our family, I had in my mind a picture of the blue tarps flying over the heads of the homeless. I thought of how willing the volunteers were to miss the last shopping day before Christmas (which is very popular with my family), how willing they were to sacrifice time, to share their talents through a crummy microphone and speaker, and in so many ways, give themselves.

I want to make sure I continue helping others. I want to be Jesus to these people. I want to do it for, and with, my kids, like my parents did with me and my sisters. I want my children to grow up as living shelters for people. Without fear.

Like any mother, I want to give my children gifts they'll remember, not just toys and things, but gifts of love and compassion. God has given each one of us unique gifts. Sometimes we act like little children, clamoring for "More!" or pout because we think someone else got a better gift. Our jealousy keeps us from seeing the importance of what we have been given, straight from God's hands. If we all shared our gifts, there would be no fear.

Only love. "There is no fear in love; but perfect love casts out fear…" (I John 4:18 NKJV). Even at Christmas.

It's my prayer that someday in the future when my children are asked to tell their memories of Christmas, they will remember something like serving in a mission with their parents, a woman playing a saw, and volunteers holding blue plastic tarps in the rain. A human portrait of a living, serving Christ.

Our Link with the Past

JANICE'S STORY

❦❦

I DUG THROUGH HUGE BOXES filled with grainy photographs, faded color Polaroids, old letters and postcards, lockets of hair, and my great-grandmother's frayed sunbonnet, all mementos of my family history. My mom sent these things from her house to mine, passing the remnants of one generation to the next. I believed it was a noble and sacred transfer rather than just a way to get more closet space. Searching through the loose photos, and undated and unchronological albums, I finally found what I was looking for—a series of three-and-a-half-inch square, glossy black and white pictures with unevenly scalloped edges. I sat back on my heels, a bit surprised by what I held in my hand. They weren't quite as I remembered them. In my mind, I had combined two or three of the pictures into one, my own revisionist collage.

In the photos, I'm five years old and grinning about the best Christmas of my life. In one, I'm mid-twirl in a long, chenille bathrobe. I remember it was pink. Beside me is a miniature ironing board with a padded cloth cover, and a tiny iron that really worked. In another, I'm seated at a small, old-fashioned wooden school desk, the kind where the top lifts up and you can put your papers and pencils inside. The lid was a chalkboard with printed letters of the alphabet across the top and numbers up and down each side. I'm seated on the attached wooden bench, partially turned to look at the camera. Well, probably to look at my mom who held the camera. I'm smiling, obviously pleased with my desk and the toy piano and the record player and all the other gifts around me.

One small feature in the photo captures my full attention. Printed in chalk on the desk are these words: I Love You. The essence of Christmas, the essence of life. I love you. My mother loved me enough to give me a wonderful Christmas. I loved her and the gifts she had given me so much that I printed the three words I knew best: I love you. An exchange of love. From a mother, *I love you,* because you *are.* From a five-year-old, *I love you,* because you love me enough to give perfect gifts. While I looked at the picture, I caught a whiff of wood and chalk dust. I nearly cried with remembering.

On the back of the photo is written: Janice, 1957. A first name, a date. Each chapter in this book begins with the introduction of a woman by the use of her first name. She is described by age, occupation, residence, personality, physical appearance, and achievement. Her story is a personal snapshot from her life. And written across each one are the words of God: *I love you.*

God's Christmas gift of *I love you* was not written in chalk but spelled out in flesh—in baby breath, tender skin, downy hair. *I love you* bound in bone and blood and wrapped in swaddling bands. *I love you* heard in an Infant's cry. A perfect gift given by our perfect parent just because we *are.*

I love you was the message given to a very young woman now known around the world by only one name, *Mary.* This Hebrew girl may have been given the popular name *Miryam* in honor of Moses' sister or as a derivative from the Hebrew word for "myrrh" or the word meaning "bearer of light." She, too, has many titles: *The Virgin Mary,* venerated as the mother of Jesus; *Theotokas,* "Mother of God," given to her by the Council of Ephesus in 431 A.D. *The Second Eve* is the title bestowed by some New Testament scholars. To me, she is *Example.*

Mary's question, "How can this be?" has been the anguished cry of many women throughout the centuries. *How can I survive this? How can I begin again? How can this tragedy be turned to good?* Regardless of our circumstance, we can believe in the angel's answer to Mary: "Nothing is impossible with God." The women in this book were willing to believe in the impossible. Their exemplary stories of trust and faith teach us to comfort and cheer one another when startled by unexpected events or unanticipated outcomes, when humbled by realities and grateful for second chances.

In the complex yet simple life of Mary, we find hope. God spoke and speaks promise to women. God was involved in Mary's life and is involved in ours. The power of God's spirit dwelt in her and dwells in us. Through her, God delivered a Savior to the world. Through us, the Savior is delivered to our spouses, children, family, neighbors, coworkers, and community. Author Barbara Roberts Pine wrote, "In her, God planted the hope of the world. In her, God found enough courage to withstand a community's scorn, willingness to endure hardship, grace enough to receive kings, and tenacity enough to flee her land for the sake of her child. Finally, Mary possessed dignity that planted her firmly before a cross where her son hung, humiliated, tortured, and howling in pain."

Mary is a worthy example of a woman who was gentle yet strong, questioning yet trusting, doubtful yet resolute, accepting yet assertive, devout yet human. The women gathered here encourage in us strength, hope, and honesty. Through their stories, they join the chorus of female voices who share the readiness to believe, the courage to ponder, and the faith to sing, "My soul magnifies the Lord and my spirit rejoices in God my Savior."

Mary's song of gratitude echoed the song of Hannah. As a young woman, she followed the scriptural example of an older woman's response. Mary's song made me wonder what I would say, what I would sing, if confronted by an angel with an unbelievable promise. Reading her statement of faith, her hymn of praise, made me wonder if I would have the presence of mind, the immediacy to respond to God with such acquiescence. My admiration of her humility, her devotion, and selflessness prompted me to write:

> If you could face your family with a countenance of grace
> If you could walk with dignity through corridors of shame
> If you could sing your soul's song to an audience of one
> Then Mary, so can I.

> If you could carry Christ into an unbelieving world
> If you could make a home for him where hope and hate both dwelt
> If you could worship your own son as Redeemer of mankind
> Then, Mary, so can I.

You pondered mysteries of eternity and time
You treasured memories of miracles divine
You cradled deity and held him to your heart
In you I find a Sister of my Soul.

Mary sang the song of Hannah, and we would do well to sing the song of Mary.

At the first outdoor Christmas concert in Bethlehem, when the angels sang only shepherds heard the song. I've always wondered how the entire town missed a heavenly host singing "Glory to God in the highest," missed the pageantry of the first noel.

Busy travelers filled the streets, anxious to be counted but dreading the tax. I wonder if they couldn't hear the celestial choir over the cacophony of their daily lives, if they couldn't see the blazing star shining above their inner darkness. I wonder if the crush of humanity numbed them to the presence of God, or if they were oblivious to the fact that Life itself was in their neighborhood, lying in a manger.

Has much changed in two thousand years? Our modern day lives are so noisy in December that we, too, can fail to hear the good news: Emmanuel! *God with us.* We are so caught up by the demands of daily life that we, too, fail to see the word of God made flesh, delivered of Mary, written in love.

In the silence of the stable, Mary pondered the astonishing events of her life, events that changed a young peasant girl into the mother of the Messiah. Women in this book have told their stories of Christmases past. Like Mary, they each found hope in the promise of God's presence. They challenge us to find a time of silence for our own reflection on how the birth of Christ affects our past, influences our present, and gives hope for our future.

I pray that our individual stories, our voices, will join the generations of women who faced life's realities but were filled with great rejoicing; women who found the courage to kneel before the Savior in a manger, women who heard the loving voice of God one silent night.

For information regarding Janice's speaking schedule, contact:

Ambassador Speakers Bureau
P.O. Box 50358
Nashville, Tennessee 37205
phone: 615-377-9100
fax: 615-661-4344
info@AmbassadorAgency.com
www.AmbassadorAgency.com

one silent night
the album

IN STORES
OCTOBER 3, 2000

A story of songs retelling
the greatest event in
the history of humankind

FEATURING SONGS FROM
LEIGH NASH, JACI VELASQUEZ, GINNY OWENS,
CINDY MORGAN, AMY GRANT, MÁIRE BRENNAN,
DA'DRA & NEE-C (FROM ANOINTED), ERIN O'DONNELL,
RACHAEL LAMPA, NICOLE C. MULLEN, CRYSTAL LEWIS

WWW.ONESILENTNIGHT.COM

MYRRH RECORDS

HARVEST
HOUSE
PUBLISHERS

Other Good Reading from Harvest House and CCM

LIVING THE QUESTIONS
by Caroline Arends

Striking a chord that resonates with anyone who has ever gone beyond the surface and touched upon the "whys" and "what ifs" of his or her faith, Arends shares pieces of her own life and walk that offer insight into why the God of the universe weaves His way into the most mundane moments of our lives. Arends shares the raw truth about a desperate summer when she could not feel the presence of God, a terrifying moment of teenage enlightenment when she discovered that she came from an "ordinary" family, and the overwhelming sense of God's majesty she felt at her first jaw-dropping glimpse of the red canyons of Utah.

BLESSED ARE THE DESPERATE FOR THEY WILL FIND HOPE
by Bonnie Keene

Bonnie shares honestly about the sense of betrayal she felt when her husband left her and her struggle to keep believing in the darkest moments of her life. As a divorced mother of two, struggling with the difficulties of parenting and clinical depression, Bonnie found hope in the healing power of vulnerability and of experiencing God's love and peace in the midst of pain. Her story is a testimony of how hope can reach us when we feel that all is lost.

RAGAMUFFIN PRAYERS
By the Ragamuffin Band/Abegg, Jimmy

Ragamuffin Prayers is a new collection of honest and searching personal thoughts on prayer by some of Christian music's most reflective artists and authors. Readers will be encouraged in their own prayer journeys by the Ragamuffin Band, Amy Grant, Michael W. Smith, Brennan Manning, Kevin Smith of DC Talk, and other popular musicians and writers as they share insights on prayer and how God uses our weaknesses and imperfections to accomplish His will.

CHILD OF THE PROMISE
by Stormie Omartian

In Stormie Omartian's joyous tribute to the birth of Jesus, the Christmas story comes to life with a fresh rendition of Mary and Joseph's journey to Bethlehem, the shepherds' awe-inspiring encounter with the Angel of the Lord, and the glory surrounding a baby born long ago in a stable in Bethlehem. Renowned artist Jack Terry has captured the poetic feel of Stormie's text with

artwork created especially for the book. The idea for Child of the Promise grew in Stormie's heart as she wrote her new Christmas musical, and the book is sure to become a favorite seasonal story to bring out time and again.